"Of course I'm upset!" Romy said

Her voice rose as she went on. "We haven't even been married a week!"

"Oh." Xavier looked as if he'd suddenly got the point. "You are jealous. But I thought you felt nothing for me?" He inquired silkily.

"It's not a question of my feelings for you," she snapped. "It's a matter of my position here in your household—the role you expect me to play. Why not invite your former lovers, too? You could start a harem!"

"The idea is interesting, but unfeasible," he purred. "I assure you, Eva is dying to meet you. And if you do not get on—this house is big enough to accommodate you both for one afternoon."

"There is no house," Romy said shortly, "that is big enough to accommodate two wives."

MADELEINE KER is a self-described "compulsive writer." In fact, Madeleine has been known to deliver six romances in less than a year. She is married and lives in Spain.

Books by Madeleine Ker

HARLEQUIN PRESENTS

HARLEQUIN ROMANCE

Don't miss any of our special offers. Write to us at the following address for information on our newest releases.

Harlequin Reader Service
901 Fuhrmann Blvd., P.O. Box 1397, Buffalo, NY 14240
Canadian address: P.O. Box 603,
Fort Erie, Ont. L2A 5X3

MADELEINE KER

KER

a special arrangement

Harlequin Books

TORONTO • NEW YORK • LONDON
AMSTERDAM • PARIS • SYDNEY • HAMBURG
STOCKHOLM • ATHENS • TOKYO • MILAN

Harlequin Presents first edition June 1990
ISBN 0-373-11274-2

Original hardcover edition published in 1989
by Mills & Boon Limited

CHAPTER ONE

THE CREAM leather settee she sat on emphasised her dark elegance, making her look both classical and exotic. She had that fine English beauty which was so unique, and yet the ultramarine blue of her eyes reflected the warm depths of a southern sea, and the hint of gold in her skin whispered of a southern sun.

She sat in a walnut-panelled room in Belgravia, watching the raindrops trickle down the row of silk-swagged windows that faced out over the street. It was a room whose style and dignity represented a great deal. Long ago, in this room and in rooms like it, she had learned to school her emotions, to preserve a calm, beautiful exterior. And that was what she was doing now, as she listened to her father.

He was not looking at her as he spoke, but was standing at the second window, hands behind his back, staring out at the same London rain.

'We thought it best not to tell you at the time, because you were very young,' he was saying. 'Just seventeen. But he had expressed an interest in you even then. He wanted to pay court to you. I asked him then if he would wait until you were older. I explained that I could guarantee nothing. I told him that you were—impulsive. A modern girl. That you would have to make your own mind up when you were an adult, when you had finished your education.' Her father paused, then went on, 'He has not referred to the subject again in the past two and a half years. But yesterday he informed me that his interest in you still holds.' Her father squared his shoulders, lifting his chin a little. 'It holds strongly.'

'I'm very flattered.' It was the very tonelessness of her voice, rather than any note of actual scorn, that made the words bite. She saw her father's hands tighten slightly behind his back.

'De Luca is a remarkable man.' Though the once-black hair had faded to silver, and the business suit was impeccably English, there was much about Ernesto Forlari that was irrevocably Mediterranean. His colouring, his accent, his build, all marked him unmistakably as an Italian. 'And he has been a good friend to us.'

'He's certainly a good businessman,' Romy said. Her voice was dry, holding nothing of its usual soft gaiety. 'So he gets me, and half the company, at one stroke? That is not friendship, Papa. A friend wouldn't be trying to make a profit out of our misfortune at this stage.'

Her father didn't turn round. 'You should not talk like that. He is offering to rescue the company from complete disaster.'

'And getting a fat slice of it, not to mention a new wife, into the bargain.' Romy looked down at her own ringless fingers. 'If I am really what he wants, why does he make our marriage conditional on his re-floating Forlari Wines?'

'That is the way he wants it.'

'Yes. The way *he* wants it.'

Romy had been shocked to the core when the family firm had gone into receivership six weeks earlier. After more than three decades at the top of the London wine-trade, Forlari Wines had been hit by a disastrous series of losses. The past few years had been difficult, she knew. A rapidly changing market had outstripped her father's old-fashioned way of running the business, and it had taken the firm too long to catch up. With bitter irony, just at the point when they were starting to make a come-back, the carpet had been pulled out from beneath them. And this year the firm, established and respected as it was, had simply run out of funds.

To her father, a man of profound honour and dignity, being unable to pay his debts had been a shocking blow. Since the receiver had stepped in, Ernesto Forlari had been like a man crushed by a burden too heavy to bear.

There was nothing she would not do for him. Nothing that she wouldn't face if it meant protecting Papa from the final blow.

But *this*——

This was something else.

'Can't we raise the money from some other source? Won't the banks help?'

'We are too far over-extended for the bank to help us.' The reply was flat and sad. 'As for the private sources of capital—you know perfectly well what the sharks would do to us. It would be worse than bankruptcy. Do not let your emotions cloud your vision, Roma. Try and think clearly. What I have said this morning may have come as a surprise to you. I doubt it. You've probably known for a long time that Xavier de Luca felt a deep interest in you?'

'I had some idea.'

'Yes. I imagined you would. Give the concept some thought, my child. You will see that he would make you a wonderful husband.'

Romy's mouth was beautiful, even when it turned down in scorn. 'Wonderful?'

'Come on, Romy!' This time it was her brother who spoke. He got up impatiently from where he had been sitting, and looked at his sister with angry eyes. Taller than their father, but just as dark, despite their English mother, Teo was looking grim. 'This is no time for coyness. What have you got against the man?'

'Just that I don't love him.'

'What sentimental rubbish!'

'Don't bully her, Teo.' Ernesto Forlari turned from the window at last, and looked at his two children with tired eyes. Romy was shocked at how worn and old he looked. 'This is not a moment for family discord. If Romy feels that she cannot marry Xavier de Luca, then we must accept that.'

'And go to the wall,' Teo snapped.

'If necessary.' Their father nodded. 'What is important is making a decision, soon. De Luca is not a man to be kept waiting.'

'Of course not,' Romy said in the same dry way.

Biting back his impatience, Teo lit a cigarette, and blew a plume of smoke upwards. 'Be reasonable, Romy. Think of us, as well as yourself. I know that to you, this arrangement may seem high-handed——'

'No,' she said coolly. 'It just seems like—an arrangement.'

'Is that so terrible?' He shrugged angrily. Six years ago, Teo himself had married, principally for the good of the business. Romy knew perfectly well that there was little love between her brother and his wife, the daughter of another wealthy Anglo-Italian family, also connected with the wine business, a girl who had brought both wealth and prestige. The marriage hadn't worked out. Yet they both seemed to accept it. Divorce didn't exist in his vocabulary.

Teo would see her present attitude—especially given the circumstances—as an unaffordable luxury.

He went on, 'Have you thought of what ruin will mean to Papa? To me? To you? You've lived a privileged life, Romy.'

'I know that,' she said quietly.

'All those smart clothes you're so fond of,' he pressed

on, ignoring her interruption, 'all the trimmings and luxuries—and that thoroughbred horse of yours—you're going to miss them!'

Romy nodded. 'Yes. I'll miss them.' But she felt little self-pity. Her compassion was all for Papa. If Forlari Wines really did vanish, consumed in the costs of receivership and paying off its debts, she had no illusions. Her father would be a broken man, disgraced and shamed at a stage of his life when he ought to have been enjoying the golden fruits of his labours.

'Frankly,' Teo added, his voice sharp, 'I'm amazed that he wants to marry you after what's happened.'

Romy looked away. There was no need to ask what Teo meant by 'what's happened'. He meant Paul Mortimer. To her elder brother and her father, her recent affair with a married man had been a severe shock. The permissive society was something that happened outside of their world. In the tradition of their family, and the circles they moved in, any woman who could not claim to be a virgin on her wedding day had very little chance of ever finding a husband at all.

Her father had been more deeply hurt than Teo, yet it was Teo whose reproaches were the sharpest and cruellest.

'He could have any woman he chose, you know,' he was going on.

'I know.'

'It's an unbelievably generous offer. You ought to be on your knees, thanking him.'

Sometimes, lately, she had the weird feeling that Teo was a stranger to her. Someone she didn't know very well at all. Did he have any idea how he hurt her when he talked like this? She kept her voice cool. 'And the share in Forlari Wines that will come as my dowry?' she asked. 'Is it generous of him to ask for that, too?'

'Do not forget,' her father said softly, 'how much money Xavier intends to sink into Forlari Wines. Enough to pay off all our debts, and float us as a going concern again.'

'But his reward for doing that will be a share in the company! What has his marrying me got to do with that? It's business, surely?'

'In our world,' her father reminded her quietly, 'business matters and family matters go hand in hand.'

'I know that.' She nodded. 'But in the circumstances . . .'

Teo snorted. 'You're trying to say you wouldn't have jumped at him, given any other circumstances?'

'I would never have *dreamed* of Xavier as a husband,' Romy said with the simplicity of complete truth. 'I can't pretend that I've never been aware of his interest, as you call it. But this morning is the first time in my life I've ever even contemplated the idea of marrying him.'

Teo's eyebrows arched. 'Do you expect us to believe that?'

'Yes.'

'Very well. And now that you've *contemplated the idea*, are you saying you don't find it in any way attractive?'

'Yes,' Romy said shortly.

'Then you're a bigger fool than we imagined,' Teo snapped.

'Perhaps it is the difference in age that upsets her,' her father said, his voice soothing. 'But ten or twelve years are very little between a man and his wife, Romy. I was almost ten years older than your mother, you know that. It is far better that the man has the necessary authority, the necessary experience. I would trust him with my life.' Her father's weary eyes were fixed on hers with an almost pleading expression. 'As for the share in Forlari Wines, he offers much in return. It is really no more than a way to cement our two families together.'

'A way of getting a damned good price for doing what he wants to do, anyway,' Romy said. 'No wonder he's obscenely rich. He has an unerring instinct for the right moment to buy—whether it's a company or a wife.'

'He is *not* buying you.' Ernesto Forlari's voice was strong for a moment. 'As Teo says, he is a man who could have any woman he chose. Think, Romy. You become a baroness, something not to be sneezed at. Your life will be wonderful! And the connection favours not only you, but our whole family, and our business. It is essential that we give him something in return, now, to balance the scales. If we do not, we will be in his debt for ever.'

'Most girls of your age,' Teo said briskly, still following his own, separate, argument, 'would be thanking their lucky stars right now. They'd be overwhelmed, bowled over. Not trying to pick holes in the man's offer.'

Romy smiled without humour, wondering whether he really believed she should be overwhelmed. 'If he could have anyone, why does he want poor little me? Why does he want to marry at all? He's having the time of his life as a merry divorcé, isn't he?'

'You must understand something,' Teo replied, more quietly. 'He needs an heir. It's common knowledge that Eva couldn't bear him children. Now that they're divorced——'

'And now that he's over thirty,' Romy interjected sourly.

Teo shrugged. 'His desire for heirs is a vital reason for his offer. It's time for him to settle down. As for the stories about him, they're all just rumour. Don't worry about the gossip-column scandal-mongering, Romy. He'll be a good husband to you.'

'A good husband?' Romy tilted her beautiful head as though considering. 'He might be. For as long as it suited him.'

'How can you be so selfish?' Teo all but shouted.

'Listen to yourself, Teo,' Romy retorted. 'You sound like something out of a play. A bad Sicilian eighteenth-century melodrama. I'm your sister, remember? You're talking about my life, not the good of the firm, or the honour of the family!'

'Your brother is upset,' Ernesto Forlari said gently as Teo turned abruptly, and walked to the window without a word. 'But he cares for you. As I do. This offer of marriage is a wonderful opportunity, Romy. I'm not talking about family honour or the good of the firm, now. I'm talking about you.' He sat beside her, laying his hand on her knee. 'When you were a little girl, I dreamed many things for your future. But never once did those dreams include the disgrace of bankruptcy and poverty!'

'Oh, Papa!' Her eyes filled with tears. 'Don't blame yourself. None of this is your fault! And what if Forlari Wines does have to close? We can start again! We'll keep the house, you said we would——'

'Romy.' The gentle tone of her father's voice stopped her. 'There would be no starting again for me. I am too old. And I would have nothing to leave my children when I died. Not even a good name.'

She felt her heart breaking. 'But, Papa, a marriage without love would be worse, infinitely worse, than bankruptcy.' She grimaced over the word. 'It will be hard, I know. But in this day and age——'

'Even in this day and age,' her father interrupted, 'it is a disgrace and a disaster. Your brother's life and your life would be ruined. After all the talk there has been about you and——' he couldn't bring himself to say Paul Mortimer's name '—you and that man, this would isolate you completely. No man of any standing would ever consider you as his wife. You would be shunned, all your prospects destroyed.'

'I don't agree with that,' she said quietly. 'But that's beside the point. The point is that I have no love for this man.'

'Do you still love the other man, the man who——' He made a brief gesture. 'The man who let you down?'

'No.' Romy dropped her gaze. It was a very painful topic, for both of them. 'No. I don't love Paul.'

'Then why do you assume that you could never love Xavier de Luca?'

'You mean apart from the fact that he's getting on for twice my age, and that he clearly feels nothing whatsoever for me?' she asked drily. 'Well, for one thing, I've been afraid of him all my life.' She thought suddenly of eyes grey and cold as a polar sea, and shuddered quickly.

'Afraid?' Her father's white eyebrows lifted in surprise. 'Why?'

'Because he frightened her once, when she was a kid,' Teo said impatiently. He flicked ash into the Murano ashtray, and leaned on the Empire desk, folding his arms. 'Ten years ago, or more. He was here on business, and he found her playing in the cellars. He picked her up and looked at her. Just trying to be friendly. She got a scare and cried her eyes out.' Her brother shrugged contemptuously. 'Stupid kid stuff.'

Her father turned from Teo back to Romy, his expression concerned. 'I do not remember any of this, Romy.'

'He did frighten me on that occasion,' Romy admitted. 'But that was just a silly incident. It's something deeper. He's always frightened me.'

'You feel some kind of antipathy?'

She countered that with another question. 'Are you so sure he wouldn't still step in to save the company—if I refused to marry him?'

'Why should he lose so much capital, and take such a risk, for a family with whom he has no connection?'

'No connection except the friendship you mentioned earlier.'

Again, it was Teo who cut in, his voice almost savage. 'You've already dragged our name through the mud with that swine Paul Mortimer! What do you want now? To ruin us all? To kill your father?'

'That's a terrible thing to say!'

'Don't you understand,' Teo rasped, 'that we're talking about Papa's life?'

'Teo, be silent,' their father snapped, but Romy had turned to stare at her father, wide-eyed.

'What does he mean?' she demanded.

'He means nothing——'

'She should know,' Teo interrupted coldly. 'Why conceal it from her? She isn't a child any more.' He turned to Romy. 'The doctors have warned Papa that his life is in danger. His blood pressure is high, and his heart is in poor condition. If you had eyes in your head, you would see just how sick a man he is. He's on the verge of a heart attack.'

'Oh, no!'

'Oh, yes,' Teo said grimly. 'He's been told that unless he reduces the stress in his life, he could be dead within the year.'

Romy stared in horror at her father's pale, drawn face. Papa would never have given her that information himself, but she knew instinctively it was true.

'Oh, Papa! Why didn't you tell me this before?' A sick pain had drawn the colour from her face. 'Why have you hidden it from me? I'm not a child any more.'

Her father's voice was quieter, more frail. 'To me, you are a child, my dear. You will always be my daughter, whatever happens. Always. And your brother had no right to tell you that.' He gave Teo an angry glance. 'It has no bearing whatsoever on what we are talking about. The person at stake here is *you*, not me.'

'If you turn Xavier de Luca down,' Teo rasped, 'I'll never speak to you again. I will know that your family means nothing to you. From now on, you would be dead to me, Romy.' He hacked sideways with his hand, as though felling a tree. 'Dead,' he repeated harshly.

And Romy, seeing the flickering tension in him, believed him. There was something in Teo, some atavistic streak of pride, that enabled him not only to say such things, but to carry them out.

Abruptly, Romy rose to her feet and walked to the desk. The eyes of her brother and father followed her, watching the exquisite, slender grace of her body, the midnight-dark sheen of hair against the silvery light. If, at that moment, she reminded each of them of another woman, a wife and mother, it was hardly surprising. Roma Forlari was very like her mother in all but colouring.

Edith Forlari had been a silver-blonde, her hair as fair as her daughter's had been dark. During her life, it had been a constant source of wonder to everyone, this white-gold mother and raven-haired daughter. But Edith had passed on her features and physique to the daughter they had named after the city where she had been conceived, Roma; the same calm, lovely face was there, the same slim, beautiful body, but coloured with a warmer palette. Had she not been born into one of the most prosperous and prestigious firms of wine-importers in London, she would certainly have been offered a career in modelling, perhaps even acting. She had the looks, the presence, to carry it off.

As a child, Romy had often heard people say of her, 'She's the most beautiful girl I've ever seen!'

But then, people said these things. And since her mother's death, almost ten years ago now, she had acquired a quiet self-possession that had somehow silenced such remarks on the speakers' lips.

Few people now told her that she was beautiful, although it was true. Few people got that close.

It was of her mother that she was thinking now, as she lifted the gilt-framed photograph that always stood on the desk. What would her mother have counselled?

That to marry a man she disliked, to save her father's business, was one thing. But to do so in order to save his life was something quite different.

She lifted her eyes from the perfect, oval face in the frame, and stared out of the window. The King's Road was cluttered with buses and taxis. Down below, a chauffeur-driven Rolls-Royce was cutting across the traffic with arrogant indifference. She could see the back seat piled high with parcels from Armani, Harrods, Mitsukiku. And the rain looked as if it might turn to snow.

He was out there, somewhere. At the Athenaeum, wasn't that his usual hotel? In some luxurious suite. Maybe even now staring out at this rainy London, waiting unemotionally for the reply to his offer.

But his eyes are so cold.

She *had* been frightened, that day in the cellars. Romy had been an imaginative child at the time, and Xavier de Luca had been a tall, rather formidable young man, who often came to stay with them, and did business with her father, and around whom she sometimes spun girlish fantasies to thrill herself. In some way, she had long ago grasped the fact of his overwhelming attractiveness to women. Perhaps she'd read it, with childish skill, in the faces of adults. The combination of attraction and fear had been very potent for her.

Which was why, when de Luca's tall figure had stooped over her in the cellars, and his strong arms had hoisted her easily upwards, so that her pale face was level with that fierce, eagle's stare, she had burst into tears.

Laughing, he had carried her out of the darkness, and delivered her to her father, who had dried her tears.

A childish incident. But one that had figured in her dreams more than once since then. Even recently, a few months ago, she'd dreamed of the fright and the tall, dark figure that had towered over her.

Now she knew why. The incident had been an omen. A sign, fraught with irony and significance.

That had happened over ten years ago. Since then, de Luca had been married and divorced. His wife had been a blonde German beauty called Eva von Schimmel, and for two years the marriage had seemed ideal.

Romy had met her on no more than half a dozen occasions. Her overriding memory was of haughty physical beauty combined with an aristocratic manner that had distinctly overawed her as a teenager. Eva had been gifted with emerald-green eyes, a large and commanding mouth that looked as though it preferred giving orders to kissing, and a facial bone structure that was worthy of a great model.

But the marriage had broken up a few years ago, and since the divorce Xavier had effectively returned to the status of a very eligible bachelor. His love-affairs had been well-reported in the press. At thirty-one, Xavier de Luca still seemed a great deal older than her. Not as old as he had seemed when she'd been a girl, but still utterly remote from her, belonging to a different generation, a faraway country, another culture.

Xavier de Luca's father and Papa had been good friends, long ago. The de Luca estates in Sicily provided some of the best wines for import, and the business connection had been established since long before the war.

The young baron, who had inherited the estate in his teens, on his father's death, had proved an exceptional businessman. She knew that her father regarded him with considerable respect.

He had been a friend of the family ever since she could remember. Tall, male and handsome, he had always had an impact on Romy. But not the sort of impact she liked. Even now she could conjure up in her memory the way he looked at her. With eyes whose authority overwhelmed her and terrified her. A disturbing, unsettling impact, a potent influence that made her sigh with relief whenever he left their house.

It made no difference in the slightest that all of her friends who had met Xavier were passionately in love with him, or that they fiercely envied her her Sicilian prince, as they called him. There was something about Xavier de Luca that she felt she could never love. 'I do not love thee, Dr Fell. The reason why, I cannot tell.' That he had wanted to marry her as long ago as two years past, when she'd been a seventeen year-old virgin, had not exactly come as a revelation to her this morning. She could even remember when it had happened.

It had been during one of his stays with them, shortly after she'd finished her A-levels. Xavier had been divorced from Eva von Schimmel for around two years at that stage. She could recall the secret conversations behind closed doors, which Teo had attended, but from which she was excluded. She could remember her instinctive understanding of what it had all been about, and remembered that even then she'd felt an ironic disbelief in the man's sincerity. So shortly divorced from one wife, how could he feel anything at all for a young girl like herself?

Seventeen! And he'd been more than a decade older! She had been nothing more to him than a girl. Thank heaven that Papa had had the sensitivity to put him off. From then on, as though acknowledging that she was no longer a child, Xavier had always stayed in hotels when he came to London. A few months later, she had gone off to Lucerne to spend a year in a finishing-school, and Xavier de Luca had faded from her mind in a happy whirl of snow, new friends, and new experiences.

The year after that, she had started a BA at university. And this year——

This year, under very different circumstances, he was offering to marry her again.

Roma Forlari, daughter of a man faced with desperation and bankruptcy, represented a very good opportunity. After all, he had married once, had loved once, and probably did not expect to love again. Therefore, the fact that she did not love him probably didn't signify. She would do as breeding stock. To give the baron his heirs.

Yet he would never, having bought her, look on her with respect. Her life might be one of humiliation and neglect. As things stood, however, that was what she probably faced in any case. That was what Teo was threatening her with.

Teo's threats wounded her cruelly. But they were not the issue at stake. Her father was the issue at stake. She had no illusions any more that this blow might damage his health permanently. She'd known that his heart wasn't strong, and that stress was dangerous to him. Teo had simply confirmed what she had already started to suspect, that Papa's health was breaking down.

Already, he had aged ten years. Teo was right. Marrying Xavier de Luca might quite literally save Papa's life!

The thought of Xavier sent a flush coursing through her veins again, erecting the fine hairs of her arms. She rubbed her skin with her palms, knowing she had to think fast, think on her feet. It was time to make a decision.

She turned to face her father and her brother. Her expression hadn't changed, but they both knew instinctively that she had somehow made up her mind.

'Well?' Teo asked urgently, grinding out the cigarette and watching her face with intent eyes. 'Have you come to a decision?'

'Yes,' Romy said quietly. 'I will speak to Xavier de Luca. Myself. Alone.'

'And what will you say?' Teo demanded.

'That's my business,' she said, walking to the door. 'You make the arrangements. I'm going for a ride.'

A thin rain sleeted down over the slate roofs of the riding-school. Huddled in her oilskin cape, Romy guided Dodo along the track from the stables towards the paddock. The big brown mare was moving with a reluctant gait. She had been warm in her stable, and now she shivered resentfully as water sleeked her glossy coat. Humans must be mad, she seemed to be saying, to want to be out in this weather.

Wet as it was, Romy needed to be out on her own, needed to cool the fire in her head and get some order back into her thoughts. She was acutely aware that these could be among her last moments of freedom. They were certainly her last with Dodo. She had decided against taking the horse to Sicily; the expense and logistic problems were too great to make it worth while. Dodo would be sold this week, and the money used for her trousseau. That was the way she wanted it.

She dismounted to open the gate to the paddock, and led Dodo through. The rich wet grass was lush underfoot, and the rain-cleansed air was sweet in her nostrils. Hauling herself back into the saddle, she started Dodo into a gentle canter towards the stand of the trees at the far end.

Was such a marriage really possible? What would her life hold with Xavier de Luca? An existence without warmth, without respect, without love. Could she sign away any chance she might ever have had of happiness, even for Papa? Maybe anything would have been better than such a marriage as this.

She let the unreality of it all wash over her. If she committed herself to a marriage with a complete stranger, committed herself to leaving her home, her family, everything she knew, and taking up a new life among people and places she knew nothing whatsoever about, what possible refuge would she have if things went wrong?

It seemed inconceivable. Yet she was trapped, caught in a complex web of duties, obligations, and family loyalties. Had she talked herself into something she would regret for the rest of her life?

Maybe she should stand up now, and tell them all she'd changed her mind. To hell with Xavier and his millions. If the price of saving the company was signing away her freedom, then to hell with the company, too.

But, if she did, what would become of Papa?

She could never turn her back on her family.

She swung Dodo round and cantered along the fence, her mouth tightening. It always came back to that. The people who really mattered to her were at stake. What other way did she have of helping them? None. Being realistic, she wasn't much use to anybody. Except Xavier de Luca.

And what would she do if she did not marry Xavier? Going back to university next term was unthinkable. After Paul, after the bankruptcy, she just couldn't face it.

What for, anyway? She would be needed at home, to look after her father. Papa would be broken, and she would have to look after him, give him all the love she could. He would need a lot of help. She winced at the thought painfully. In any case, her education just didn't mean that much to her any more. She would take it up again, later, if she wanted to.

She rode for nearly an hour, until both she and Dodo were hot and panting with the exertion. A few rags of red and gold marked the sun's grave in the west. Feeling the ache in her back and loins, Romy knew it was time to quit. Utterly depressed at the prospect of going back home, she guided Dodo back to the gate.

As she rode back to the stables, she knew with complete certainty that the afternoon's thoughts had just been dreams. There was little consolation in 'what-ifs' at this stage. She *was* going through with it.

What other choice did she have?

The rain did turn to snow, after all.

Later, staring into the mirror at Eaton Square, she went through the whole thing again, her thoughts quick and cold, deliberately without emotion. There must be room in de Luca's bargain for her own requirements.

She was not looking forward to meeting him tomorrow. Not looking forward to looking him in the eyes and making her demands. It occurred to her that he hadn't seen her since last year, on his last visit to London. He probably hardly remembered what she looked like any more. Behind her own image in the mirror, she saw another face, or rather, the ghost of a face. A male face, extraordinary in the intensity of its grey stare and grim, forbidding mouth. Hair like hers, black as midnight. A mask of power.

Romy was restless as she rose from the dressing-table

and walked to the small ivory-tinted bathroom that opened off her bedroom. She showered and washed her hair, thinking for the first time in days about Paul, the man she had once imagined she'd loved, and who had changed her mind about love for ever.

A handsome, gifted man a few years older than Romy, he had been sent on an eight-month course at the university by the international firm who employed him. They had met by chance, and the attraction between them had been instant and warm.

It was not hard to understand why Paul had hidden the fact that he had a wife and two-year-old son in Scotland. He had been—or had imagined he'd been—utterly bowled over by Romy. Rather than risk losing her, as their London University friendship deepened into an affair, he had chosen to conceal the fact of his wife and child.

She herself had been unbelievably foolish. She had never questioned his need to go back to Scotland without her every weekend without fail—to put in time with 'the firm'. It had troubled her that Paul seemed so reluctant to involve her in his family life—or, for that matter, to become involved in hers—but she had accepted his story that his parents were ill and cantankerous, and that a meeting with them should be shelved until later.

She had been too absorbed in the development of her first real relationship with a man, and too inexperienced in the ways of the world, to see how deceitfully and dishonestly Paul was treating her.

She'd been appalled when she'd found out. Paul's fraught admission that he was already legally committed to a wife and a two-year-old child had brought her cloud-castle crashing down around her ears.

The final touch had been Marianne's, Paul's wife's, declaration that she was suing for a divorce, and would be citing Romy as her husband's adulterous lover when she filed her suit with the magistrate.

Paul, in the midst of this ongoing catastrophe, had wanted to keep pretending. Pretending that after the divorce he would marry Romy, that they would live happily ever after in a Bohemian heaven.

But the scales had fallen from Romy's eyes with a vengeance. Her family, inevitably, had found out everything. Shame had affected them in different ways. Her father's silent anguish had been, in many ways, harder to bear than Teo's rage. Until Marianne's reconciliation with her husband, and the dropping of the divorce suit, they had lived through some very dark days. In her darkest moments, she sometimes even suspected that worry about her had been one of the reasons for her father's finally losing his grip of the business.

Oh, yes. Paul had made them all suffer.

In retrospect, she could find it in her heart to understand, but not to condone. It had hurt her more painfully than she could have dreamed. The impact on her sensibilities had been savage. It was as though she had been stunted in some way, as though a tender plant, just putting out its first flowers, had been exposed to a killing north wind.

Her emotional life, she knew, had been effectively brought to a halt for several years. It would be hard, if not impossible, to recover from what Paul had done to her. She had already schooled herself never to expect to be happy again.

Xavier de Luca could not love her, any more than Paul had done. She had to resolve, right now, to get whatever she could out of the marriage for her own family, if there was to be a marriage. She anticipated that she would have to give him an heir, but that need not imply any emotional contact.

And Teo had been partly right. The impending bankruptcy had affected her life deeply, just as Paul's betrayal had done. Between Paul and the bankruptcy, her expectations of the future had changed for ever. Material security was the best she could hope for, for herself. For Papa—for her beloved father—she could do something more . . .

The telephone interrupted her thoughts, and she picked it up, wrapping her towel around her naked body.

'He'll see you tomorrow morning.' It was Teo's voice, calling from the warehouse. 'Ten o'clock, at the Athenaeum Hotel. I'll take you over.'

'I'll drive myself.'

'It'll be easier for you if I pick you up,' he urged. 'I'll just drop you off outside the lobby. He'll meet you in the conference room.'

'How appropriate,' Romy said drily. 'OK. Pick me up here at around nine-thirty.'

'Romy——' Over the phone, Teo sounded younger, more like her brother and less like something out of that Sicilian melodrama '—this is your big chance. *Our* big chance. Don't——'

'I won't do anything silly,' she interrupted. 'Don't worry.'

'It would make things a lot easier if we knew what you were going to say to him.'

'I think that's my business,' Romy said gently.

'What I mean is, don't blow it, Romy. This could be the most important decision you ever take. Don't forget how powerful this guy is——'

'I know how powerful he is. You don't have to explain.'

'And you know what Papa's state of health is——'

'Don't be brutal, Teo. I know that, too.'

'Right.' Then, as though wanting to apologise for his

harshness earlier today, but not knowing quite how, he added gently, just before he rang off, 'Take care of yourself.'

CHAPTER TWO

ONE THING at least, that Romy knew was how to dress with style and grace. She put on make-up first, knowing she was using too much. But she wanted no chinks in her defences today, and, if the beauty she achieved was almost masklike, it satisfied her need to feel protected.

The clothes she chose, too, suggested disguise, protection. The jacket was heavy, its black crêpe panels like Japanese armour. Broad shoulders had been the hallmark of the Milanese collection from which it had come, adding a hint of strength to her slender figure. Beneath it she wore the fitted suit in charcoal wool that always looked so sombre, with a white silk blouse to set the deep colours off.

Black suede court shoes, a black suede handbag and, as a final thought, black leather gloves completed the ensemble.

When she looked in the mirror she saw only a woman's oval face, framed in darkness. The scarlet mouth and the glint of deep blue in the eyes were the only touch of colour against the sombre clothes.

Well, let him be under no illusions about her. Just as she would cherish no illusions about him. Let him see that she had refused to dress so as to titillate or flatter his male ego. But just before she went down to meet Teo she lifted the heavy rope of Italian gold out of her jewellery box. It had been her eighteenth birthday gift from Papa. Around her neck, it added a golden gleam to her darkness, rich and opulent—to remind him that, rich as he was, the Forlaris were also not without pride.

When Teo arrived to pick her up in the silver Jaguar his eyes widened.

'What's the matter?' she asked tersely, sliding into the hide seat. 'Do I look wrong for the occasion?'

'You look——' He studied her with something like awe. 'You look very beautiful. But not nineteen. You look like someone else.'

Romy smiled curtly. 'Shall we go?'

As he eased the car into drive, Teo's expression settled back into impassivity.

The Athenaeum was a relatively small hotel, but its location was impeccable, and its views across Green Park—now so strewn with snow that it was White Park instead—were beautiful.

A pin-striped sub-manager was waiting in the foyer to meet Romy and lead her upstairs to the conference room where she was expected.

Teo kissed her cheek. 'Your face is like ice,' he murmured. 'Are you all right?'

'Yes,' she nodded, taking a deep breath.

'Ask the reception to ring for me when you're ready. And be careful.'

He hurried out of the foyer without further advice, as though glad to get away. Her heart was suddenly beating heavily and painfully inside her. Romy turned to the sub-manager. 'I'm ready.'

'This way to the lift, Miss Forlari. Autumn's well and truly over, it seems. We're in for more snow tonight, so they say on the television.'

'Do they?' She hardly listened to his inconsequential chat about the weather as he escorted her up to the fifth floor, and led her down a plushy carpeted corridor.

There he opened an oak-panelled door for her, bowed, and waited for her to go in.

It was a smallish room. The windows were draped so

that its contents, an oak table and twelve chairs, were softly, almost poorly lit. As she walked slowly through the door, the first thing her eyes met were the dozen empty chairs, and for a moment she thought the room was unoccupied. But as the door was closed behind her she saw the man standing at the far end of the room; and with her heart in her throat she walked noiselessly across the dove-grey carpet to meet him.

Xavier de Luca made no effort to come forward. He simply waited, leaning casually against the windowsill. His pose was relaxed, and yet undershot with a rocklike calm which gave her the weird feeling that he had been waiting there for her not for minutes, but for years.

Silhouetted against a shaft of wintry light, he was a figure without details. A figure so familiar to Romy that she would have recognised his outline in a glimpse across a crowded square; yet now, as she stared at him, she was seeing him with new eyes, with a new knowledge, with new emotions.

He was very tall, tall enough to tower over her, just as he had done all those years ago. But the sliver of light from behind the curtain illuminated wings of silver in the black hair which hadn't been there ten years ago, and the shadowy face showed lines of mature authority. She didn't need to see his features, though, to feel the presence which surrounded him. A blind woman would have sensed that magnetism.

Romy paused in front of him, her mouth dry, her chest tight, and looked into the shadowed eyes. She sensed a gaze that brooded on her, that seemed to look through her surface, into her depths, as though all this morning's girding of loins had been in vain.

He did not speak. Slowly, Romy brought her hands together, and finger by finger pulled the black leather glove from her right hand. Then she held it out to him, and said in a quiet voice, '*Buon giorno, Signor Barone.*'

He took her hand. His voice was deep, with a slight rasp that might have been characteristic, or might have suggested irony.

'*Buon giorno, Roma.* I thought you never spoke the language of your fathers?'

'I speak fluent Italian,' she said levelly. 'But I prefer to speak English.'

'Then we will speak English today.' He released her hand. 'Please sit down. Will you join me in a cup of coffee?'

She nodded, obeying his command to sit. He did not follow suit, however, and she found herself staring up at his dark figure. He touched a bell on the wall. The waiter must have been poised outside the door, because he entered almost at once with a silver coffee-set, poured for them both, added cream at Romy's request, and exited in complete silence. The Baron de Luca obviously had a talent for making things go smoothly around him.

What light there was in the room now shone in her face, hiding his expressions, but making hers visible.

The first thought she'd had on seeing him, the thought that was still swirling around in Romy's head was—what does this man want with me? As her eyes grew accustomed to the soft light, she could make out more details: not just the exquisitely cut suit, but the aggressive male energy of the body that wore it; the hardness that it could not disguise. Not just the watchfulness of the grey eyes, but the formidable intelligence that glittered in them. This was a man, fully mature and dangerous. Beside him, Paul had been a child, a half-formed boy. What could she ever hope to achieve against that frightening strength?

She sipped the coffee, the rich cream coating her tongue, going down almost queasily into a stomach that was tense with nerves. He took his sugarless and black, gulping it down in Italian style.

'I did not expect snow,' he said, nodding at the veiled windows. 'I left Italy in warm sunshine, the trees heavy with autumn fruit.'

'In England, snow tends to come early,' she replied with a shrug. 'And it tends to stay a long time. This is a freak, but it sometimes happens this way.'

'I prefer the Italian climate.'

'Most people do. But you get used to English weather.'

'More coffee?'

'No. And I didn't come here to talk about the weather,' she added tersely. 'Neither of us did. I'd like to dispense with the small-talk, if you don't mind.'

He glanced at her briefly, though she could not make out his expression, and poured himself a second cup. 'No, I don't mind.'

'Then let's get down to business.' Nerves had made her voice brittle, so that she sounded hard and assertive.

'Business? If you like to call it that.' His voice was husky, slightly accented, a deep voice that gave everything he said a special quality that was not quite hostile; mocking, perhaps. He sat opposite her, the piercing eyes meeting hers. 'Very well. Presumably your father has conveyed my offer to you?'

'Yes.' She nodded.

'Do you accept?' he asked, almost casually, drinking the second cup more slowly.

'I have a counter-proposal to make,' Romy replied, picking up her discarded glove and folding it.

His expression seemed to be politely enquiring. 'Indeed? Go on.'

She launched into the initiative brusquely, the way she'd planned to do last night. 'To start with, I cannot accept your offer if it includes your taking a share in

Forlari Wines.' She stiffened her voice still further, trying to sound emotionless. 'I fail to see any relevance in that clause. It places an unacceptable burden on my family. And it demeans me.'

He crossed one leg over his knee with a rustle of fine tailoring. 'In what way would it demean you?'

Her beautiful mouth curved momentarily downwards in an expression of distaste. 'It would make me feel as if I was being . . . bought.'

There was the hint of a dry smile, which might just have been a trick of the light. 'And aren't you?'

She controlled her temper. 'No. A proposal of marriage is a social contract, not a business one.' Her eyes were very wide as she spoke, framed by thick, dark lashes. 'I could never accept an offer that gave a stranger any rights over my father's business.'

'But perhaps your father thinks otherwise,' Xavier de Luca said, smoothing the natural rasp of his voice. 'Or do you speak for him?'

'I speak for myself. If you want me, Xavier de Luca, then you must be prepared to pay the full price for the merchandise.'

There. It was said. But there was no reaction from the figure in front of her. He continued to watch her expressionlessly, but said nothing, so she plunged on. 'I will marry you on one condition: that you give my father, as a gift, with no strings attached, the full amount you spoke of investing in the company. There will be no question of your owning any share or rights in Forlari Wines. Otherwise, there's no deal.'

'Go on.' The voice was pure rasp now. Was he angry? She'd expected an outburst, but this quietness was worse.

'Go on? What more is there to say? You have heard my offer. Either you accept or you refuse!'

'I refuse.'

Shock silenced her for a moment. 'You refuse?' she repeated in an altered voice.

'The price is too high.' He leaned back, one hand tapping the arm of his chair negligently. 'Far too high.'

'But how much is a wife worth?'

'That depends on the wife,' he replied smoothly. 'Have you any idea of the amount of money required to get Forlari Wines going again?'

'No,' she said shortly.

'Let's say that half a million pounds would not be an extravagant estimate.'

Romy felt sick. She hadn't known that the sums involved were anything like so huge. No wonder Papa had been looking so shattered. She kept her feelings out of her expression. 'Very well. Then half a million pounds is the sum we are talking about.'

Xavier tilted one eyebrow. 'What do you have on offer that is worth half a million pounds?'

'Just myself.'

'Ah.' His eyes were distantly amused. 'Just yourself.'

Her mouth was a stubborn line. You cold-blooded bastard, she thought. She sat up straight, her breasts tautening against the black crêpe, making his eyes drop momentarily to take in their smooth swell. 'You want an heir,' she said clearly. 'I am capable of giving you one.' She challenged him with slender eyebrows, and he made a brief movement with his hand.

'I imagine there will be no problems,' he said.

'There won't be. I'll give you two children. You have a right to expect that from a wife. And surely each child is worth a quarter of a million to a man of your wealth?'

'If you care to put it like that. You seem to have very definite ideas about all this.'

'I have.' She nodded grimly. 'After I've given you your children, our physical relationship must end. I'll live wherever you want me to. I'll be your wife in all other senses. But once your second child is christened, we will no longer be . . . lovers.' Her eyes glimmered like sea-water in a marine cave. 'Lovers, for want of a better word.'

He had not moved, but she thought she could sense the gathering anger in him. There was certainly an ominous glitter in the eyes that had never left her. It was only with a supreme effort that she finished her carefully rehearsed speech. 'Of course,' she continued, 'you can't be expected to live like a monk.' It had become almost unbearable to keep holding that piercing gaze. 'So the best solution is probably for you to take a mistress. I imagine you have one now . . .' She slapped the loose glove against the palm of her hand, a nervous, defiant movement. 'I don't know. I don't care. I will raise no objections if you keep her. Or any number of mistresses, as you please.'

This time there was a positive reaction, though it was hard to say exactly what it was. It was like the flicker of lightning against a grey sky. Or a shiver of muscle under a hunting panther's fur, over before it was even sensed.

'And this is the offer you came to bring me this morning?'

A hundred years ago, she thought suddenly, this man could have had me killed with a snap of his fingers. Had she gone much too far? She'd thought all this out last night. Last night, in her mind, it had sounded businesslike, reasonable. Today it had come out harshly, and she knew that his feelings had been abraded. What were his emotions now? Disgust? Anger?

He rose abruptly from his chair, and flung the heavy curtains away from the window behind them. The room brightened painfully, making her wince. The wintry light was dazzlingly white, bleached by the heavy snowflakes

that danced against the panes. She looked up at de Luca,
seeing him in detail for the first time.

If his expression had not been tight with anger, he
would have been incredibly handsome. Handsome in an
almost frightening way.

Everything about Xavier de Luca seemed to be
embodied in his face. The supreme confidence that
stemmed from centuries of arrogant dominion, wealth
and power marked the lines of black eyebrows and a
deeply cut, harsh mouth. The stormy grey eyes, narrowed
now as they stared at her, contained flecks that turned to
gold when he smiled, or silvered when he grew angry.
Right now, they were chips of ice, and the expression in
them turned her heart over inside her.

The tanned skin around his eyes was creased by
uncompromising lines, spreading into the silvered
temples, curving down into the high, strong cheekbones.
Around the mouth, too, lines curved up to the arched
nostrils—lines not of weariness, but of experience,
marking a bronzed, vigorous face with mature
masculinity.

The dark eyebrows were heavily defined, expressive,
curving half-way round the deeply set eyes in a way that
gave his expression a permanent intensity. They almost
met in the middle, evidence of a formidable will. His
mouth was rich with passion and drama, deeply carved
and arrogant.

The sort of man you met only once in a lifetime.
Instinctively you knew that the lean, hard body would be
beautiful naked, constructed with the same spare,
dangerous grace as his face. Fine, strong hands contained
the same male power; the one he leaned on was clenched
into a veined fist, as though he would have liked to strike
her, and send her sprawling on this beautiful carpet in
tears.

'Naturally,' he said, his voice jagged, 'you discussed all this with your father before coming to me this morning?'

She drew a deep breath. He must know that his physical appearance would daunt her, but she was damned if she would show it. 'No, I did not. I have my own mind, Baron de Luca. This is my business.'

'And mine,' he said pointedly.

'Only if you want to make it your business.' Her hands were shaking, and she clasped them more tightly. 'The choice is yours.'

She watched with a lump of ice in her throat as he slowly unclenched his fist and rested it on his hip, pushing aside the jacket to reveal a taut waist hugged by a silk waistcoat cut in Sicilian style.

'And you have no feelings one way or the other?' he asked, clipping the words contemptuously.

'Yes, I have feelings.' She looked away from his eyes. 'And I have pride, exactly as you do.'

His eyes glittered. 'So it seems.'

'I want my father to enjoy the rest of his life. I don't want him to die despised and poor, of a broken heart. I want security for my family. All I ask is that you provide us with that, in the context of an arranged marriage. In exchange, I am offering you two children, heirs for your estate. And I offer to be a good mother to them.' She looked at him directly. 'I just don't want any hypocrisy or any pretence. Doesn't that seem like a fair proposition?'

'Fair?'

She coloured at the cutting tone. 'May I remind you that it was you who sought me out, not the other way round. I am not the one seeking this marriage. Had circumstances been otherwise, I assure you that I would never have contemplated you as a husband!'

'Am I so repulsive, then?' he enquired.

'You are well over ten years older than me,' she

reminded him in the same frigid tone. 'But I intended no insult, Baron. I know quite well that you enjoy considerable success with women.'

Romy rose to her feet as she said the words. She made a sketch at a smile, but it contained only tension. 'And now, I'm sure you will want time to consider what I have said. There isn't much else to discuss.'

'Not on your part, perhaps.' Fingers like steel gripped her wrist, the ungloved one, as she turned to go. 'Wait,' he said softly, pulling her without apparent effort to face him.

She lost her balance for a moment, taken by surprise by his strength. Involuntarily, she put out a gloved hand to steady herself against his chest. Through the scented leather, through the silk of his shirt, she felt hard muscle, and the contact, the physicality of it, made her cheeks flame hotly.

'Let's go through it once more, this offer of yours.' She submitted to being held captive by him, her face still flushed, her eyes veiled by long lashes. He spoke quietly, in that husky, dry voice. 'You feel I am not entitled to a share in Forlari Wines. You want me to refloat your father's company out of my own pocket. You expect me to support you in a certain style.' His eyes dropped to her lips. The perfect leaf of her mouth was parted slightly as she breathed faster, showing the milk-white line of her teeth. His fingers tightened cruelly around her wrist as he went on, 'You will condescend to be my lover—for want of a better word—until you have given me two children. After which duty, you will no longer have to put up with my attentions. In consolation, however, I am permitted to keep any number of mistresses if I want to. Now, have I got all that straight?'

Romy bit her lip hard. 'I see I've been too blunt for you. I'm sorry that you're angry.'

'Don't be.' He released her wrist, and she rubbed it, seeing the angry red marks on the pale flesh. 'Why should I be angry, in any case?' he went on, his voice becoming silkier. 'You have been extremely honest with me.'

Romy glanced at him, caught unawares by his apparent change of mood. Slowly, she began pulling the glove back on. 'I wanted to be realistic,' she said coldly. 'You made a blunt proposal. I felt it needed a blunt reply.'

'Your attitude is extremely mature for a girl of nineteen.'

The knowledge that he was mocking her made colour rise to her pale cheeks. 'I'm old enough to know my own mind,' she retorted. 'Old enough to understand what this kind of marriage would be.'

'And what would it be?' he enquired, folding his arms.

'Just like all marriages. A convenient arrangement whereby a man imprisons a woman while remaining free himself.'

'Is that what they taught you at university?' he asked satirically. 'You remind me of a certain fox—or should I say vixen?—and a bunch of grapes. What is out of reach is always sour.'

'What's that supposed to mean?' Romy demanded.

'Your relationships have not been dazzlingly successful so far, have they?'

The words were like the flick of a lash on raw skin. Romy looked up at him hotly. 'You've heard about me and Paul, then.'

'I made it my business to hear. Was it because you despised the institution of marriage that you picked a married man?' His eyes glinted. 'Or was adultery some kind of turn-on?'

'I didn't know he was married,' she gritted, trying to keep her temper. 'Why should I defend myself from you?

It's common knowledge that you're no angel where women are concerned! And anyway, having been through a divorce, do *you* have a normal outlook on marriage?'

If she had hoped to disturb the infuriating composure that sat on his handsome face, she was disappointed.

'Having been through a divorce,' he repeated, eyelids drooping lazily. 'You make it sound like Sodom and Gomorrah.'

'It explains why you're here, anyway. Your first wife couldn't give you children. That's partly why you divorced her, I imagine. Now, as you get older, you're starting to think about leaving your estate and your title to the next generation. So you find you need another wife, one who can give you the heirs you want.'

Xavier de Luca stared down at her with hooded eyes. Were it not for the enduring sting of his fingers on her wrist, she would have found it hard to believe this man had any emotions at all. 'How perceptive of you. But this does not explain why I have chosen you, out of all the women in Europe.'

'Oh, I think it does. At first, when you heard that my father was going bankrupt, I bet you got your pen out to cross me off your register of eligible spinsters.'

His mouth moved in a mocking smile. 'But then I stopped, pen poised over the page?'

'Yes.' Without answering the smile, she went on, 'You stopped. The more you thought about it, the more you realised that here was an opportunity to get all you wanted, and more.'

'Do explain,' he said in a velvety voice.

'Does it have to be explained?' she shrugged. 'You could present yourself as the saviour of the hour, putting my father and brother under a heavy obligation. Instead of paying a dowry, as would be the Sicilian way, you could buy yourself a very nice wedding present. A fat slice of Forlari Wines.' Her eyes flashed. 'Your pious attitude doesn't fool me, Xavier. I may not have a head for business, but even I know that half a million pounds is a very cheap price to pay for half of Forlari Wines. Once the company is refloated, you'll make back that investment in four or five years. After that, it will all be pure profit. And you'll have gained a suitable young wife for breeding stock into the bargain.'

'Really,' he drawled, shaking his head, 'your insight is quite disconcerting.'

His callous mockery sparked off some sudden devil in her own soul. Romy felt the angry words rise to her lips and spill out. 'Did you really think you could get away with it? My father may be a sentimental innocent, and my brother is too greedy for his own good, but I'm different. I see right through you, *signore!*'

The snow gave way for a moment, allowing a ray of wan sunshine to come through the window. It touched her as she spoke, giving her hair the iridescence of a raven's wing. For a short while he continued to stare at her, the flecks of ice in his eyes seeming to burn with pale fire. Romy felt her hands shaking, her stomach churning with emotion.

Then he turned away, and walked to the window, staring out across the park. The moment of sunshine faded back into gloom, and a flurry of snow beat against the windowpane in front of him. Without turning back to her, he said in a quiet voice, 'You say you do not want any hypocrisy or pretence. Don't you think hypocrisy and pretence are the common coinage of most human relationships?'

'That's cynical,' she said sharply.

'Practical,' he corrected. 'A certain amount of what you call "pretence" in our marriage might help make life a little easier to bear.'

'You mean that you want me to pretend I like you?' she scorned.

'Other women have not found that so difficult.'

Romy looked at his back. He was supremely male, supremely attractive, the kind of man whom most women found irresistible. A man with a face and body like his would live in a heady atmosphere of female adoration, and could probably not begin to count the number of his conquests, physical and emotional, over women. The combination of threat and sexuality in his manner would be irresistible to most women.

But did he really expect her to succumb, like some eager society flirt bored with her husband? Lively anger danced in her eyes. 'I am not "other women", Baron. I care nothing for you, just as you care nothing for me.'

'I care enough to propose marriage,' he said drily.

'For your own reasons. I'm honest, at least. I prefer the truth to any number of lies, no matter how pretty. I don't want to quarrel with you, or offend you,' Romy said, making an effort to tone down her voice. 'If we both play by the rules there's no reason why we can't both get what we want. My brother used an appropriate word. He called it an "arrangement".'

'An arrangement.' At last he turned to face her, his expression somewhere between amusement and contempt.

'That's what it is,' she said, looking up at him, calmer now. 'An arrangement between two intelligent, adult people.'

He slid one hand into his pocket. 'Intelligent and adult?' he repeated, in a voice that made her wince.

'Yes.' Romy nodded. 'I can see that you think me cold and hard. It's in your eyes.' She looked down. 'I'm just trying to see my future clearly. I will love my children. But how can I ever feel anything for you? And how can you ever feel anything for me?' She glanced up, her eyes narrowed. 'Have no illusions. Please, I warn you. The truth is, Baron, that you and I have both lost the capacity to love. There is nothing left for us but a marriage like this one.'

He stared at her for a moment, eyes like flints. Then, again, a slight smile crossed his face. 'Are you really nineteen?' he asked gently. 'There are things about you, Romy, which are very old. But then, the very old and the very young do sometimes share the same crystalline vision, unclouded by sentiment. And perhaps you're right. Perhaps that is all we are left with. I accept.'

Romy felt the breath leave her lungs, as though she'd been plunged into iced water. In a tight voice, she asked, 'You accept everything?'

'Yes.' It was said calmly. The smile was gone.

She could only stare at him with parted lips. Had it really happened, then? With an effort, she asked, 'You'll give my father the money? All of it?'

'I have said so.' He nodded. In the silence that followed, Romy felt her emotions swell, ready to explode into tears that might have been of grief, of relief, or both. She fought the passions back fiercely, and the only sign of their passing was a misting of her eyes.

Xavier de Luca watched her dispassionately. If he noted the tears in her eyes—and he could hardly have failed to see them—he made no comment. Instead, he took a crocodile-skin cheque-book from the inside pocket of his jacket, and sat down in front of her, a gold pen poised to write.

'There are a few areas to fill in,' he said, 'so let's get them over with. Your relationship with Paul Mortimer—may I ask how it happened?'

'You probably wouldn't understand the first thing about it, and I don't intend to explain,' she said haughtily. 'Let's say that he was unbelievably weak, and that I was unbelievably stupid.'

'Yes,' he agreed drily, 'let's say both those things.' His contempt was so patent that Romy flushed dully, ashamed for herself, and ashamed for Paul. 'How long were you lovers?'

'A term.'

'How long is that?'

'Long enough to get involved,' she said briefly. 'Not long enough to really know someone.'

'And this relationship—which you think I could never understand—is at an end, then?'

'Yes.'

'Permanently?'

'Permanently,' she ground out. 'There's something you should know about my relationship with Paul Mortimer.'

He looked up at her. 'Go on.'

'It changed me.' She took a deep breath. 'I was very much the naïve innocent before—before it all happened. I'm not any more. I've learned a great deal about human relationships from Paul. You may think me cold and calculating, but I've been through a hard school. And I don't intend to let another man take advantage of me. Not ever.'

He stared at her for a long while, his eyes assessing. 'Very well. And now there's something you ought to know about *me*. You have said that I can take a lover once sexual relations between us have ceased. But I will never permit you that licence. If you are ever unfaithful to me, Roma, I will divorce you immediately. Is that understood?'

There was no mockery or equivocation about his tone now. Her cheeks a deep red, Romy nodded stiffly. 'I understand that.'

'The Italian courts,' he said, eyebrows lowering ominously, 'will ensure that you are left with nothing. Not even your children. You may find that you are never allowed to be alone with them again. You accept this condition?'

'I find it insulting that you should have to mention it,' she replied coldly. 'But I accept it, yes.'

He considered her flintily. 'You will probably have given me my heirs before you turn twenty-five. After that, you will no longer sleep with me, and you will not be allowed a lover. You seem to have no difficulty in signing away your sex-life from then until the day you die.'

The words sent a chill through her, but she lifted her chin slightly. 'Whatever you may think of me,' she replied with spirit, 'I'm not promiscuous. And abstinence is easy for a woman. It is men for whom it's a penance!'

'Indeed?' His expression was ironic.

'In my experience, that's so.'

'In which case, I bow to your vast knowledge.' Her cheeks stung with colour, as though he'd slapped her. 'Your father will have explained the other conditions attendant on our marriage. You will live in Sicily, in my home at Luca. You will always be with me. I will never allow you to take up a separate residence. You understand?'

'Yes,' she said huskily, hating him for the way he was treating her.

'My life-style is well-settled,' he went on. 'It will make no concessions to your whims or wishes. I will expect you to be at my side wherever I travel, and to be present at whatever engagements I undertake.' He gave her a wintry smile. 'Apart from being what you have so neatly described as *breeding stock*, you will be expected to take your full share of my social life. You will entertain in a style which is suitable to your rank, and you will see that my households are run efficiently and smoothly.'

'I think I can manage not to disgrace you,' she said disdainfully.

'You know nothing,' he said flatly. 'You have a great deal to learn. I do not expect you to become a perfect wife and hostess overnight. What I *do* expect is willingness to learn.'

'I'm quite sure,' she said acidly, 'that you'll find me a great disappointment after your first wife. But if you want me to play the part of the grand lady, then yes, I will do my best.'

'Above all,' he said, eyes narrowing slightly, 'I require one thing from you. Obedience.'

He paused, as though to let the word sink into her brain. Romy said nothing for a moment. Her eyes glanced at the gold pen poised over the cheque-book. Then she swallowed. 'You have a right to ask for my co-operation,' she said huskily. 'But obedience—that's another thing.'

'Yes,' he said grimly. 'Quite another thing. But that is what I require of you, Roma.'

She gave a painful smile. 'What else do I have to lose? I will obey you, *signore*.'

'Then we understand one another.' He wrote with brief, decisive strokes, tore the cheque from the book and handed it to her.

It was made out to her father, and it was for five hundred thousand pounds.

Romy took it numbly, unable to speak or think clearly.

'I will deal with your father from now on.' He rose, and she followed suit, feeling her legs weak and trembling.

'My father?'

'To discuss the wedding arrangements. I'd like everything settled as quickly as possible. I hope you don't want anything elaborate?'

Romy's mouth tightened. 'That would be hypocritical.'

'I intend to ask your father to keep any reception to a minimum.' He walked away from her, towards the door, as though the things they'd been discussing had been of little consequence to either of them. He opened the door on to the corridor, then looked back at her. The tanned face, etched with the bold lines of those formidable eyebrows and the downward-curving slant of the authoritative mouth, was like a warrior's mask. 'Was there anything else?'

'No,' she said in a low voice. 'Nothing else.'

But as she walked with him to the lift she was filled with turmoil. At the lift, the lump in her throat threatened to dissolve into sobs. She had thought herself so very much in control back there. For a while. But he had dominated her in a way that had shaken her. She'd been unable to match his incisive intellect or his unexpected shifts of mood and tone. Which of them had really won? What was she letting herself in for, on this snowy autumn morning?

De Luca took her limp hand, and raised it briefly to his lips. The gesture was a formal one, carrying no warmth, and anyway, she couldn't even feel his lips through the black leather. 'I shall leave you here, Roma. I see little reason for us to meet before our wedding day. But if there is anything else you wish to discuss, you know where to find me.'

She nodded, unable to speak.

Then the stainless steel doors were opening, and she was stepping into the little prison of the lift, fumbling for the buttons. Her last glimpse was of his eyes, grey and flecked with silver.

Then the lift doors closed, imprisoning her.

CHAPTER THREE

KATHERINE DRUMMOND'S voice carried across the roomful of chatter. 'Oh, the man is utterly, irrevocably gorgeous,' she fluted, inhaling the bouquet of the pale-gold champagne as though she were an expert—which she was, being a senior partner in one of the biggest wine warehouses in the West End.

Romy, politely listening to an elderly De Luca cousin who spoke only Italian, and was one of the few members of the groom's family to have come to the wedding, glanced across the room at Xavier. He was talking to Laura Forlari, Teo's wife, who had proved an invaluable maid of honour to Romy that morning, and there was no doubt that Katherine Drummond was right. There was not a man in the room apart from her father who could match the impact of his looks. Beside his dark strength, all the others looked pasty.

Like the male members of her family, he was in a morning-suit, a white rose at his lapel. The black brows were knitted slightly, as though he were concentrating on what Laura was saying to him. But he was also wearing a slight smile, and Romy was sure that only she, of everyone present, could detect the faint irony in his eyes.

He was so tall that Laura, a petite woman, was compelled to turn her face up to him, almost like a child. Her cheeks were flushed, and her eyes were star-bright with an excitement that was obviously due to Xavier's proximity.

Xavier caught her glance over Laura's shoulder. The grey eyes jolted her, and she saw him nod imperceptibly, as though he had read her thoughts, as though confirming her opinion that this was a charade, a play in which only they two knew the true script.

She turned away, feeling the flush of his contact drift hotly through her blood, and murmured an assent to whatever it was the de Luca cousin was saying.

Katherine Drummond's voice drifted through the hubbub again. She was talking to everyone and no one, and she didn't seem to care that Romy could clearly hear her words across the drawing-room. 'But that only deepens the mystery. As far as I know, she has only met the man a few times in her life. And yet here they are, getting married out of the blue. Then there's the age gap. She's a lovely girl, but hardly in his generation, is she?'

'Perhaps it's one of those Sicilian arranged marriages,' someone suggested in a quieter voice. 'They tend to do things in the old-fashioned way, you know.'

'Old-fashioned?' Katherine smiled obliquely. 'Forlari Wines is out of receivership all of a sudden, did you know?'

'You mean——?'

'I mean that a large capital injection has been administered in just the right place. Do you think the gorgeous Baron has been stung?'

Romy felt the small, dry smile rise to her lips. She was fully aware that conversations like Katherine Drummond's were being repeated all around the room. Even among the noisy group of her own friends, chattering at the far end of the room, she'd caught the whispers and speculative glances. Yet she was glad of the reception. Relatively small as it was, in deference to Xavier's wishes, it was staving off her departure with her husband.

She was married.

She stood here, the Baroness de Luca, her future in the

hands of the man who stood a few feet away, an utter stranger to her.

The wedding had been quiet but beautiful. The church had been filled with scented flowers, and there had been only the closest family members in the congregation. The society photographers had been there, of course, waiting outside in the whirling snow, and she'd held her smile in place as the icy flakes had scattered her hair and clothes with diamonds. Her friends had thrown confetti, and her sister-in-law had cried.

It had taken an enormous effort to get through it, so cool and poised.

She heard her father's laugh from across the room, sounding light-hearted for the first time in months. His expression all day showed how he'd been bursting with pride at his daughter's wedding.

Poor Papa. He was so convinced she was doing the right thing. When she'd told him she was going to marry Xavier, his eyes had been moist with joy. He didn't have the slightest idea of what a cynical, loveless arrangement she'd come to with de Luca. Neither he nor Teo had any real understanding of the bargain she'd struck with Xavier. She knew they preferred to think there was some romantic desire for the match on her part, and she knew that the truth would have appalled them. They also thought that refusing to take a cut of Forlari Wines was a spontaneous gesture of generosity on Xavier's part.

She snorted. The idea of Xavier de Luca doing anything generous would be amusing if it weren't so bizarre.

She excused herself from the elderly de Luca cousin, making her way across to where Katherine Drummond was standing.

She had lost weight over the past couple of weeks, and looked all the more exquisitely elegant for it.

She'd refused point-blank to indulge Xavier's desire that she wear a long white dress with a train. The key-note for her outfit had been off-white. The cream suit was impeccable, with a short jacket of ravishing prettiness. She'd set it off with pale tan shoes and gloves, and a small cream hat with a little careless sketch at a veil.

It conveyed indifference to the occasion, a kind of cheeky and defiant gaiety.

'A beautiful outfit for the races,' as Madame Leclos, her couturier, had remarked, 'but somehow *impertinent* for a wedding, darling!'

Well, she'd wanted to show impertinence! She hoped that the same gaiety was reflected in her expression, though she knew that the Mediterranean blue of her eyes had darkened to an Adriatic ultramarine, and the hint of gold in her skin had faded to ivory. But perhaps people would put that down to the snowy weather, or the excitement. The classical beauty of her features was unmarred by any emotion as she arrived at the group.

'Hello, Katherine,' she said lightly. 'Hello, everyone. Thank you all for coming to my wedding.'

The round of cheek-kissing and the choruses of 'you look lovely, darling' lasted a few minutes.

'I suppose we shall have to call you *Baronessa* from now on.' Katherine smiled as the compliments subsided. 'If you ever get tired of him, darling, toss him my way, will you?'

'He's fabulous,' one of the other women gushed, looking over her shoulder at Xavier. 'We were just saying that none of us had ever seen you with him before. How long have you known him?'

'Almost all my life,' she answered truthfully. 'He's an old friend of the family, though he doesn't come to London all that often. His father and mine were close friends.'

'And were you promised to him, darling, long ago?' Katherine Drummond's eyes scrutinised Romy sharply behind the smile. 'Was it all arranged in high Sicilian style? A childhood betrothal? Names scratched with a diamond on the library windowpane?'

'Something like that,' Romy agreed calmly. It was as good an interpretation of the truth as any other.

'How romantic.'

'Yes,' Romy said brightly. 'My husband is a very romantic man.'

'So it seems.' Katherine savoured the vintage champagne appreciatively. In her late fifties, she was still unlined, the taut skin of her face scorning the mechanics of a surgical lift. 'Though I'd never imagined you as the deeply traditional type. I thought you were such a modern young thing.' Her catlike green eyes drifted across to Xavier, the expression in them veiled by drooping lashes. 'You've kept your handsome betrothed very dark, Romy.'

'Well, now you can feast your eyes on him.' She smiled coolly. Which was exactly what most women in the room were doing. The glances they gave him were devouring. How many would be envying her, longing to be in her place? An acute sense of the satirical overtones of the situation kept her smile in place. If only they knew . . . She turned to one of the other women in the group. 'I haven't had a chance to thank you for the beautiful candlesticks, Sheila. They're exactly the kind of thing I love.'

'Glad you like them.' Sheila Davis, a couple of years older than her, was flushing slightly. She was a handsome blonde woman who had been her childhood playmate. Sheila and her husband were among the only people who had given presents today; Romy had made it clear in the short period leading up to the wedding that she didn't want any gifts, but inevitably some of the guests had either ignored her request, or had been mixed up. Sheila was one of the latter. 'I know you like Georgian silver, so David and I . . .'

Her voice tailed off faintly as Xavier materialised beside Romy, smiling down at them from his considerable height. 'Candlesticks,' he repeated in his deep, husky voice, his eyes on Sheila. 'Are we indebted to you for those charming silver candlesticks?'

'Just a little thought,' Sheila said breathlessly. Always slightly fugitive, she was now clutching her elbows and flushing painfully under Xavier's gaze. 'We got sort of mixed up about you not wanting any presents . . . do hope we haven't given any offence . . .'

'Please.' With bone-dissolving courtliness, Xavier had taken her hand, and was raising it to his lips. 'It was a most generous gift, and my wife and I are infinitely grateful to you.'

'Let me introduce you to everyone,' Romy said drily, watching Sheila's melting eyes and scarlet cheeks. She went through the names without fuss, taking a quiet private amusement in watching the various sets of female eyes react to Xavier de Luca. There was something very amusing about being the only woman in the room completely indifferent to his charm.

Or, at least, apparently indifferent.

Since that meeting at the Athenaeum, she'd had enough time to school her emotions, to cultivate a shell around her feelings. She'd made her choice, and the important thing now was to see it through without weakness. The pearl-like culmination of her preparations was this afternoon's cool poise, this well-contained appearance of indifference.

'And you fly to Sicily tonight?' someone was asking her.

'At six.' She nodded, feeling her stomach turn over as she said the words.

'To the family castle?' Katherine Drummond asked Xavier.

'It's hardly a castle,' Xavier said easily. 'Just a rather rambling old house. Though it's true there is a Norman tower.'

'It sounds deliciously romantic,' Katherine cooed. 'But then, the whole thing seems like a fairy-tale to us dull English. Romy has just been telling us about how she was betrothed to you as a child. We never suspected! One would have though arrangements like that had disappeared in the nineteenth century . . .'

'Indeed.' Xavier's grey eyes glanced at Romy's face with veiled sarcasm, but he neither confirmed nor denied the tale for Katherine's benefit. Instead, he smiled into her eyes. 'Whatever arrangement it was that brought me such a beautiful young bride, I can only thank my Fates for it.' She felt his fingers close round her arm. 'I want a word with you,' he murmured in a lower voice. They excused themselves, and walked towards the fireplace, where a pile of logs was crackling against the autumnal snow outside.

Conscious of many eyes on them, Romy looked up into his tanned, dark-browed face impatiently. 'What is it?'

'I have not yet had a chance,' he said softly, 'to tell you how beautiful you look today.' The stormy grey eyes glinted with a mockery that was sexual, dangerous. 'I am sure that every man in the room must want you. As I do.'

Damn him. Romy's mouth tightened to hide her reaction to the compliment. 'Is that what you took me aside to say?'

'Partly.' He nodded.

She stared at the magnificent face. 'Then please get on with the rest of it,' she said briskly. 'This is my last day with my friends and my family.'

There was some mean gratification, at least, in seeing the amusement fade from his face.

'Very well,' he said. 'The rest of it is this—the weather is worsening.' She glanced involuntarily out of the window. The murky sky could hardly be seen because of the swirling snow. 'I have just spoken to air traffic control at Heathrow,' he went on. 'There is every indication that our flight will be cancelled by tonight. But there are still seats on the next flight to Rome, in two hours' time.'

'I don't understand.'

'We must go. If we leave now, we will just make the afternoon flight.'

'Now?' She looked at him with angry blue eyes, feeling her nerves tighten. 'You mean—just walk out of my own reception?'

'The alternative is to be snowed up here for several days, possibly a week,' he pointed out. 'I cannot afford that. I have important engagements to fulfil, Romy.'

'Isn't this an important engagement?'

Lines curved round his cold smile. 'I have an estate to run in Sicily. I have already been away for longer than . . .'

'Longer than necessary to get this insignificant little matter sorted out?' she supplied sourly as he hesitated.

'I was going to say longer than I expected.' He shrugged. 'But perhaps it comes to the same thing.'

'Then perhaps *you* should get the afternoon flight,' she replied shortly, 'and I'll follow when the weather clears.'

The tough masculine lines of his cheekbones and chin hardened as he clenched his teeth. 'Don't be absurd,' he rasped. The impact of his displeasure shocked her like a slap. 'You are my wife now. Where I go, you go.'

'But I——'

His eyes glittered. 'You agreed to obedience—

remember? This is where you start, my love. I did not take you aside for a discussion of the situation. I am *telling* you that we are leaving now. It is time you made the announcement.'

Romy reached out to one of the massive wooden candlesticks on the mantelpiece, as though grasping for support. He meant it. Her voice was strained. 'But how can I leave all my guests standing—and Papa and Teo——'

'I have already explained to your father and brother,' Xavier cut in. His eyes were as wintry as the weather as they stared into hers. 'They understand completely. So will your guests. Now, will you make the apologies, or shall I?'

The ice-flecked gaze held hers like iron, and Romy felt her will bend like a bow, not quite breaking. For a few seconds longer she looked into his face, seeing no weakness, no yielding in so much as a line of it. She was in the mood for a fight, boiling to hit back at him.

But to make a scene here, in front of her family and guests, was inconceivable. She clenched her teeth to bite back the sparkling words of anger. 'As you wish,' she said in a low voice.

If he gloated over her capitulation, he showed no sign of it. 'Good. To coin a phrase, please get on with it.'

The colour had left Romy's cheeks, and she knew she was as pale as her dress as she turned to the room and began to speak.

'Please listen, everyone . . .'

There were 'aah's of disappointment, and a scattering of ribald comments from the younger guests as she finished. She saw her father and Teo both staring at her, their eyes, so alike, holding identical expressions of sadness.

They had been so eager to marry her off to Xavier de

Luca, she thought. Perhaps they had only just begun to realise that their solution would mean they would lose her, conceivably for ever. Faintness overwhelmed her.

She felt her husband's strong arm around her, and for the first time was grateful for the contact. She was feeling suddenly very weak and dizzy.

'I sincerely regret having to drag Romy away from you all,' he said, his slightly accented voice carrying easily round the room. 'But you can imagine how eager I am to have her . . . all to myself.'

There was more laughter. Xavier went on to make a brief, elegant speech of thanks and farewell. Her legs were weak as he escorted her to her family.

'You must hurry,' Papa said in a low voice, taking both her hands and kissing her cheek. His calm, she knew, was only a controlled cover for his emotions. Odd, she thought numbly, how Italians were supposed to be so emotional. Papa was one of the most self-disciplined men she knew. 'We will say goodbye later, child. Get ready now, and Teo and I will see to the guests from now on.'

'Your bouquet.' Laura was kissing her cheek, and putting the bouquet of lilies into her arms. 'Don't forget it, *cara*. And don't forget to throw it to the spinsters. *Quell' uomo*,' she sighed dreamily, shaking her head. 'What a man! He's going to make you a fantastic husband.'

'He's had plenty of practice, at any rate,' Romy heard herself say distantly. 'This is his second time round, Laura.'

Leaving the room, amid a general noise of goodbyes and well-wishing, Romy was hardly aware of what she was doing or saying. So many people who wanted to touch her, kiss her, press some last wish for happiness on her. So many familiar faces that she might never see again.

'Have you much to pack?' Xavier asked her

unemotionally, in the hall outside.

She shook her head, shivering. 'J-just my overnight bag. Ev-everything else is d-done.'

'Good.' He wiped a solitary tear from her cheek with his thumb. 'Go upstairs and get ready,' he ordered quietly. 'The taxi will be here in five minutes.'

She obeyed numbly, feeling more lost than she'd ever done in her life. Time was seeping away. The last grains of sand were trickling out of the hour-glass.

Saying goodbye to her father and brother was almost unbearable. It was only the iron presence of Xavier at her side that stopped her from dissolving completely.

The crowd of guests had spilled out into the icy air, taking shelter from the weather under the Corinthian portico of the house. As she broke from her father's embrace and hurried blindly to the waiting taxi, there were cheers, and another hail of confetti and rice, hardly needed in the swirling snow. She barely remembered to fling her bouquet to her friends, saw someone's gratified expression as she clutched the cream lilies to her breast. Then Xavier was helping her into the taxi.

She waved at the window, struggling to send a smile to Papa and Teo. But between the snow and her tears all she could make out was a dancing blur of light.

And the taxi was pulling away from the kerb, carrying her away from the house of her girlhood forever.

They had arrived at last.

Feeling drained to the last drop of strength, Romy sank down on to the carved bench with the embroidered cover. She huddled into her fur travelling-cape, and closed her eyes. The feeling of unreality that came with travel, exhaustion and new places was starting to blur her senses.

The weather had caused endless delays with their flights. They had spent silent hours beside one another in various airports. That they had been respectfully steered away from the common herd, and put in VIP lounges, had made little difference. Waiting was waiting, Romy had discovered, whether the seats were plastic or plush, whether the drink was ersatz coffee or French champagne.

By the time they had reached Rome, the attitude of airline officials towards Xavier had become almost obsequious. A title, she'd thought drily, obviously still carried considerable weight in republican Italy. For a while it had seemed that they would not get away from Rome, and that she would be spending her wedding night in the Hilton there. But the snow had eased off for half an hour, long enough for the flight to be hustled into the air. In the soft light of the first-class cabin, she'd felt sleep sweep over her.

It was well past midnight by the time they'd arrived at Catania airport in Sicily. A pearl-grey Daimler limousine had been waiting on the tarmac, complete with liveried chauffeur, so that they hadn't even needed to go through the airport building. Some invisible but effective prior string-pulling had ensured that their luggage was the first to emerge. The chauffeur had loaded it into the limousine, and they'd been speeding away in warm luxury before the weary crocodile of ordinary passengers had even reached the terminal.

It had taken another two hours to drive from the airport to the house. By now they had left the snow behind them, but the night was starless, and it was cold and windy, as though building up for a storm.

Somewhere in the house a door crashed shut with the wind, making her start dully and open weary eyes.

How very different from the English elegance of her own home. The hall she sat in was vast. At the far end, a huge fire had been lit for them in a stone fireplace big enough to roast a whole ox in. The walls, elaborately panelled in stucco plasterwork, were hung with rows upon rows of paintings, some dim and obscure with age. Everything gave the impression of belonging to another era. It hadn't escaped her attention that the immense crystal chandelier that hung from the beamed ceiling had never been converted for electricity. It carried perhaps two hundred thick wax candles.

The furniture was all antique; not the glossily restored chi-chi antiques of a Kensington mansion, but massive and ornate and baroque, imposing in its splendour. She had just washed in a marble-walled downstairs bathroom, where the gold fittings had gleamed, and an alabaster statue had smiled enigmatically down at her.

This was her home. Too many details to take in, too much beauty and grandeur for a tired mind to grapple with.

'Do you want to eat?'

She looked dully up at Xavier, who was standing over her, and shook her head. 'I'm not hungry.'

'Then you must have a drink. Come by the fire.'

She rose tiredly, and walked down the long room with him to the huge fireplace. Several servants were busy taking their luggage upstairs, and another, an elderly man with grey hair, was putting out a silver tray of drinks by the fire. He bowed as Xavier approached, and kissed his hand.

Xavier introduced him as Sergio, the major-domo. She knew he was a person of importance in the household, and she summoned up a smile for the elderly servant. Inwardly, she was wondering how many hundred years into the past she'd travelled tonight.

The heat of the great fire had made her fur coat superfluous, and Xavier helped her off with it. She felt the warmth of the flames lick at her cold body. Xavier had poured her a glass of wine. Their fingers touched as he passed it to her.

'Marsala,' he said. 'Drink.'

Romy usually had no taste for the sweet, heavy stuff, but right now it was exactly what she wanted. It spread soothing fingers through her weary limbs, smooth and mature as honey. With a little groan, she sank into the leather wing armchair.

'You must be tired,' he said, watching her dispassionately.

'Yes.' She took him in with dark eyes. He, at least, showed no signs of wear. The austerely handsome face was as composed and controlled as it had been hours before, at their wedding. The same expression of concentration was in place as he looked down at her. 'I don't understand why you aren't exhausted, too,' she said languidly.

'I am used to the journey.' He refilled her glass. She drank the second Marsala like medicine, sighing as she felt the alcohol slide down.

'It's been a long day. Can't we go to bed now?' she asked.

'In a moment.' He nodded. 'They are unpacking the luggage in our bedroom.'

She glanced up at him quickly. '*Our* bedroom?' The implications made her deep blue eyes suddenly widen.

'Your days of sleeping alone are over, Romy. Had you forgotten?' he asked in his husky, mocking way.

'No.' She bit her lip quickly to stop it trembling. There was one more ordeal to face before this endless day was over. The most difficult ordeal of all, the only part she had really dreaded.

'You have not enjoyed today, have you?' he asked.

She looked up. 'Enjoyed?' she echoed drily. 'What was there to enjoy about it?'

'The ceremony. The reception.' He sat on the arm of

her chair with a rustle of fine material, and she flinched as his warm fingers touched her temples. 'It's usual for women to enjoy their wedding day.'

'You're the expert on weddings,' she retorted, making drinking an excuse to turn her face away from his caress. 'Did I disappoint you?'

'You behaved rather like a spoiled child,' he said with a glitter in his eyes. 'I hope that's not going to be your usual response.'

'I am simply being myself,' she said in a cool voice. 'I warned you not to expect anything different.'

He smiled slightly. 'You made a beautiful bride, at any rate.'

'I'm glad I pleased you in that, at least.' She drained the glass. 'And you? Did you enjoy the day?'

'I hope it may yet improve,' he said softly.

She looked down, letting the empty glass droop from her fingers like a tired flower. At the lip of her glass, a heavy drop of wine had gathered. Following her eyes, Xavier reached out, and gathered the drop on the tip of one long finger, then carried it to her mouth. Romy closed her eyes as his finger caressed her lower lip gently. 'Surely,' he said softly, 'you can no longer have any virginal fears about the marriage bed?'

'No,' she said, barely audibly. The wine was sweet on her lips. 'I've got no fears.' But she had started trembling, and her heart was pounding dully in her ears. She'd never felt less prepared for anything in her life. The fact that she'd already had one lover in her short life didn't diminish the impending trauma of submitting to his lovemaking. She put the empty glass down, and twisted her fingers. 'Let's get it over with.'

He rose, tall and broad, and offered her his arm. 'Yes,' he agreed. 'Let's get it over with.'

Supported by him, she got to her feet, and let him

guide her to the wide, dark staircase.

There was another fire burning in the bedroom, bright enough to light the wide four-poster bed with a flickering glow. There was no other illumination. In the shadows, she could see that flowers had been placed everywhere, and their sweet fragrance was in the air.

Some servant had unpacked her bag, and had laid her plain white cotton nightie out on the left side of the bed. Her hairbrushes and toiletries were on a dressing-table, and her little doeskin slippers were on the floor at her side of the bed.

Xavier tossed his coat on to a chair and came to her. She stood unmoving as his arms encircled her, the hard warmth of his body closing against her. The warm aura of the man enveloped her.

For a few minutes he simply held her, caressing her with slow, sensual fingers, as though to ease the tension out of her muscles. 'You are my wife, Romy,' he whispered huskily. 'Mine at last. I have been waiting for this moment for a long, long time.'

His mouth sought hers, his lips warm and hungry. His kiss was warm and passionate, but Romy made no effort to respond. Why should she pretend a passion that she did not feel? Her skin was like marble, and as her cold lips yielded to the pressure of his desire she closed her eyes. Her arms hung limply at her sides, not moving to embrace him. His kiss grew cruel and angry at her lack of response, and he broke away.

'What's this?' he asked tersely. 'Are you a woman made of stone?'

'What am I supposed to do?' she retorted, flushing. 'Fawn and kiss my master's hand, the way the servants do?'

'You could at least behave like a normal woman!'

'I keep warning you to have no illusions,' she said in a

tight voice. 'Why won't you listen? You knew what you were taking on when we spoke in that hotel room.'

He stared at her, his eyes glittering. 'Yes,' he said. 'I knew what I was taking on. Perhaps my approach is wrong.'

Xavier moved to her again. His fingers invaded her hair, pulling her face roughly to his. As she gasped in shock at the sudden violence of it, Xavier's mouth closed on her own. It was a kiss of almost cruel sexuality, his tongue pressing against her teeth, thrusting past them into the sweetness of her inner mouth.

There was a quality in the roughness of the kiss which stirred something inside Romy, stirred some passionate response. She felt the fire awaken in her body, an impulse that made her press momentarily against him, arching her throat to taste the tongue on her palate. Her hand was on his chest, the thudding of his heart just beneath her palm. Weariness left her, to be replaced by a rush of heat.

The kiss burned for brief seconds, like an opened furnace door.

Then, swiftly, self-awareness came to her rescue. Furious with herself, rather than with him, she thrust away so violently that his fingers caught in her hair.

'*Don't*,' she said fiercely. But he had felt her moment of response, and there was a smoky smile on his mouth now.

'You enjoyed that,' he said softly.

'No!'

'Yes,' he contradicted her. 'Is that the way you want to be wooed? With roughness and force?'

'I don't want to be wooed at all,' Romy said, her face a pale mask but for the dark blue of her eyes and the hectic red of her mouth. 'That's a fiction we can do without, Xavier.'

'You insist that our relationship is hostile?' he asked, lowering his brows.

'I refuse to pretend,' she retorted. 'You held my father to ransom to get me. You used the cruellest kind of blackmail. You played on my family feelings to make me agree, and if I hadn't fought back you'd have ended up with half the company as well!' Her eyes were sparkling with contempt. 'Does your vanity really require me to pretend that I'm going to enjoy any of it?'

'You're distorting the reality,' he snapped. 'There was no question of ransom or blackmail.'

'It seemed that way to me!' The points of her breasts were hard and tender. 'In any case, isn't it enough that I've agreed to fulfil my side of the bargain without opposition?'

'Without opposition,' he repeated silkily. 'With what, then? Complaisance? Submission?'

'Anything you like.'

'Anything I like, except volition.' Two or three strands of her hair were still wound round his fingers, and he drew them off. 'But male sexuality is a strange thing, Romy.' His voice was drily mocking. 'It relies on more than complaisance from a woman. Call it vanity, if you wish. But something more than submission must be present. Some indication of desire. No man can make love to a woman whom he knows does not want him.'

'I don't believe that,' Romy said disdainfully. 'Men go to harlots, even though they know they cannot truly want them.'

His smile died, and displeasure spread ice through his eyes. 'Harlots at least take care to pretend. But in any case, I was speaking of lovemaking, not animal sex.'

'And I was speaking of animal sex,' she rebutted, 'not lovemaking.' Her beautiful face was strained. 'I agreed to the former, not to the latter. Why the hell should *you* care, anyway? You're obviously not over-delicate in your tastes!'

'What is that supposed to mean?'

'Oh, come on! You have as many women as you feel like! Your flirtations and amours are well-known, Xavier.'

'Your tastes are evidently not over-delicate, either,' he retorted, tight-lipped. 'I had a short interview with Paul Mortimer before the wedding. Is that trivial little mannikin really your ideal of manhood?'

'He has sensitivity, at any rate,' she flared.

'The sensitivity to betray two women at the same time?' Xavier ground out. 'How could you have given yourself to an unscrupulous little worm like that?'

'Please,' she said with shaky irony, 'your primeval Sicilian jealousy is showing, *signore*. I'm just asking you to show a little diplomacy.'

'Diplomacy?'

'It might be kinder if you . . . waited until I'd settled in a little before . . . claiming your rights,' she said, her tone an awkward mixture of defiance and plea. 'Perhaps a more sensitive man might understand better.'

He shrugged brutally, not even considering the idea. 'You are my wife now, Romy, not Paul Mortimer's mistress any longer. It seems to me that the sooner we start a normal marriage, the better for both of us.'

'You like that word, don't you?' she said with a twisted smile to cover her disappointment that her hopes had just been dashed. '*Normal.* But there's nothing normal about this marriage. Why must you try and pretend that there is?'

'Nothing is normal about any aspect of life,' he retorted brusquely. 'Everything is abnormal that isn't grey and flat.'

'I realised long ago that you can have no real interest in me,' she said with disdainful irony. 'It's a waste of time for you to pretend that you feel anything else.' She turned away, bracing herself. 'But I'm not drawing back from my part of the bargain. If you want to assert your possession of me that badly, I'm always available from now on. You bought me this morning, remember?'

'Don't talk like that,' he said sharply.

'Why not?' she challenged. 'It's better than talk of wooing and loving. Don't worry, though. Tonight you can do with me as you choose. I won't stop you.'

Suddenly she was aware of an arctic anger in him. 'You arrogant little——' Luckily for her, he didn't finish the sentence. 'Do you really think you're so overwhelmingly desirable?'

'You don't understand . . .' she faltered, taken aback by his vehemence.

'You've been desired by one man, and now you imagine you're some kind of queen,' he cut through roughly. 'Who the hell are you, that you think you can treat me with such presumptuousness?'

She was shaken. 'I simply want——'

He turned away abruptly. 'For pity's sake,' he grated in a dry voice, 'stop arguing, take off your clothes and get into bed. I have no intention of forcing you against your will.'

'I simply want to get things straight between us,' she persisted, her throat dry.

'Things are straight enough. Do as I say,' he commanded brusquely. 'And please don't say any more. I've heard all I want to hear from you tonight.' He was already stripping off his shirt, so violently that she thought she heard stitches rip. He flung it away, walking towards the bathroom. She caught a glimpse of a superbly muscled back in the light as she door closed behind him, and then she was alone.

For a moment shame burned in her. The fact that she didn't have to endure his lovemaking was small consolation, now.

But she was too drained to sustain any sentiment for long. The weeks of tension were taking their toll now. She undressed numbly, letting her feelings ebb away. She preferred this anaesthetised dreaminess, at least, to any emotion that she might feel tonight. The sheets were cool and welcoming. As she laid her cheek on the fine linen, she had the strangest feeling that she was falling, slowly but without pause, into shadowy depths.

She was almost asleep, her mind drifting on dissociated thoughts, when she felt Xavier slide into the bed beside her. His body did not touch hers. He made no move to reach for her, and she made no move to reach to him. There was to be no lovemaking tonight. Exhaustion overwhelmed her. When she closed her weary lids again, she could see Papa and Teo's faces. All her past was behind her, now. There was only this strange present, with this dark stranger . . .

Feeling nothing any more, Romy waited for it, too, to slide into the black abyss.

CHAPTER FOUR

ROMY awoke alone. In the air were the mingled scents of flowers and the dead fire in the grate. With a yawn, Romy rolled to the edge of the bed and sat up stiffly. She ran her fingers through the black tangle of her hair, feeling that she must look utterly awful this morning.

Not surprising, after yesterday.

Xavier had obviously arisen hours ago. The impression of his body was still there beside her, and an empty coffee-cup was on his bedside-table. She thought back to last night, the events now as unreal as a dream, and grimaced. She'd fully expected he would take her last night, forcing his dominion on her whether she cried or not. But he hadn't. With hindsight, she should have gone through with it, got it over. That way she wouldn't have to think about tonight.

In the pale morning light, she saw that the bedroom had been decorated in beautiful shades of faded crimson. It was a lovely room with three arched, mullioned windows on each of the side walls, its noble proportions enhanced by the choicest antiques. Someone had arranged several vases of white and red lilies around the room, and it was their scent which made the air so fragrant.

Distant household noises reached her from behind the carved oak door. If the lovely gilt clock on the mantelpiece was to be trusted, it was five past ten.

She got up and walked to the centre of the three windows on her side. Leaning on the sill, she stared out at her new surroundings.

Directly below, a formal rose garden was enclosed by a hedge of closely clipped yew. There were stables and outbuildings to the left, backing on to a row of tall, ancient cypresses, their walls of faded peach and cream, their roofs of burned orange tiles. A sloping hillside of olives stretched into the middle distance, separated from the orderly rows of a vineyard by another row of silvery grey conifers. She could see sheep grazing under the trees, and the brown figures of perhaps a dozen horses among them.

Further away two dozen pretty farmhouses clustered into a small village, smoke rising from their chimneys. They, too, wore those characteristically Mediterranean colours of bleached pastel walls and ancient terracotta roofs, but their smart green shutters bore testimony to the fact that they were far from rundown. All around the village, fields of wheat and huge vineyards spread. A lorry piled high with bales of hay was trundling down a distant road. And beyond, the sea.

It was only a mile or so away, a sheet of deep blue under the heavily clouded sky. Romy glanced over her shoulder. Through the opposite row of windows, an oak forest stretched towards a craggy mountain range. The house was situated, then, between the hills and the sea.

Right now, she would have given all this foreign beauty for a breath of London air, for a glimpse of a busy London street, for a word from her father . . .

A gentle tap at the door interrupted her moment of melancholy. The maid who came in to the room, wearing a smart black and white uniform, had a solemn expression.

'My name is Concetta, *Baronessa*.' She folded her hands shyly. 'The master has told me to attend to you from now on. Would the *Baronessa* like a bath?'

'I'd love one.' Romy nodded, wondering just what 'attend to you' meant.

'With bath oil?'

'That would be nice. And . . . could you possibly help me wash my hair first?' she asked. 'It got into such a mess last night.'

'Of course, *Baronessa.*' The maid was already going to the bathroom and stooping over the bath to turn the taps on. The delicious scent of tuberose bath oil wafted out on a cloud of steam as she emerged again.

'What will you wear today?' she asked, opening the cupboard and turning a pretty face to Romy. 'It is cold,' she warned. 'The warm weather has gone.'

'Oh . . .' Romy surveyed the perfectly hung rows of her clothing. 'The grey plaid skirt, with a blouse. And a cashmere jersey.'

With quiet efficiency, the maid was putting out the clothes, effortlessly picking a jersey the right colour to go with the skirt, and laying out three or four scarves for Romy to choose from. She was probably about the same age as Romy, and Romy wondered for a moment whether she had served Xavier's last wife in the same way; then she dismissed the thought. Concetta was too young for that. This expertise had obviously been acquired in the more recent years since Eva had left, tending to a succession of mistresses.

Wincing sourly at the thought, Romy realised that the sensible thing was obviously to get used to the situation as soon as possible. There was no going back home now.

Wreathed in towels, she sat in front of the basin while Concetta deftly wet the thick black sweep of her hair, and began to massage in the rich shampoo. The clean smell enfolded Romy, redolent of summer.

'That smells lovely,' Romy said, inhaling the spicy scent.

'It has oil of rosemary in it,' Concetta nodded. 'Also laurel, and civet. It is very good for black hair like yours.'

As Romy submitted luxuriously to having her hair washed, Concetta kept talking, assured now that her mistress was in the mood for conversation. The Sicilian dialect she spoke was very different from the classical Italian Romy had learned in London. It was sometimes difficult to understand, but she managed to follow the gist of it.

The village, Concetta said, was called Luca, hence Xavier's family name. The family owned the village. Yes, *owned*. All the land for miles around was part of the vast estate, which was mainly agricultural. Some of the biggest vineyards in Sicily were here. That was where Xavier was now, checking that the immense property was in good order after his long absence.

As for the house, which she called *il palazzo*, it dated from the ninth century. The master bedroom and this bathroom were actually in the tower, which had been added in Norman times—hence the arched windows. Magnificent dances and parties were held here, she said, though not so many since the divorce.

Concetta fell silent after she'd said that, as though wondering whether she'd broached an indelicate subject.

Romy, relaxed into dreaminess, opened her eyes slowly. She thought of that other woman, and hoped that Eva de Luca's wedding night had been more auspicious than her own . . .

'She was a good hostess, I imagine?' she asked.

Concetta massaged Romy's hair briskly. 'Oh, yes. *La signora* Eva loved to have people here. There were always big parties, big dances. She knew how to entertain; she was a woman who was always laughing, always gay.'

'She sounds rather ravishing,' Romy said with a hint of dryness. 'It's a pity I can't take lessons from her.'

'I am sure you will see her soon,' Concetta assured Romy, missing the irony in her mistress's tone. '*La signora* Eva has a villa on the coast, at Lipari. It is only a few hours on the *autostrada*. She and the master often see one another.'

'Often?' Roma repeated in a cold little voice.

'Yes, indeed. They are not like some divorced couples, who are enemies. They remain quite close.'

Then why did they get divorced? She couldn't stop the brusque question from forcing its way into her mind. Was there someone else? Did he have affairs? These were not the questions she could ask a servant.

Romy bent her neck so that Concetta could rinse away the rich lather, and digested what she had heard in silence. The maid's firm hands squeezed the excess water out of her hair, then wrapped it neatly in a towel. 'I will make the bed, *signora*, while you bathe.'

Her hair wrapped in a cocoon of fluffy white towel, Romy stepped into the bath, and sank with a little gasp into the hot, fragrant water, then sighed as her skin adjusted to the temperature.

'They are not like some divorced couples, who are enemies. They remain quite close . . .'

Something about that idea was just not palatable. An inner voice told her that she would be meeting *la signora* Eva in the not too distant future, and that the encounter would not be an easy one. She had anticipated problems, but not problems of this sort. Not getting on with your husband was one thing. Finding yourself in competition with a woman like Eva von Schimmel, a former wife into the bargain, was quite another.

Competition? Who was she kidding? There *could* be no competition. Eva had known Xavier for years. Her relationship with him was established, had that depth and intimacy that only time could bring. It was Romy who was the incomer.

She was starting this marriage with more disadvantages and handicaps than she knew how to deal with.

She washed and rose dripping from the bath to dry herself. Reflected in the mirror was her own naked body. She glanced at the full, high breasts, the sweepingly graceful lines of firm flesh, and the long, elegant legs. The arc of delicate collarbones framed a slender throat, supporting a face that was beautiful and thoughtful.

But right now, her own beauty was no consolation, and she reached for the pale gold silk gown. Why hadn't Eva gone back to Germany? Why was she still living in Sicily, within a few hours' drive of Xavier?

Aware of another presence, she turned with a little laugh, pulling the gown around her.

'Sorry, Concetta. I was just thinking——'

But it was not the maid. It was her husband.

The words died in her throat as she met Xavier's eyes. The silk gown was unfastened, and his gaze dropped to the starlike point of one uncovered nipple, dropping even further to assess the curve of her hip and thigh. Flushing a feverish scarlet, Romy covered herself.

'It's customary to knock,' she said hotly, wishing intensely that he hadn't seen her like this.

'Not in my own house.' He walked up to Romy, and brushed a stray tendril of hair away from her brow, making her flinch away from the contact. The piercing eyes raked her face mercilessly. 'This morning, I watched your face while you slept,' he went on in a soft, husky voice. 'I had not realised what a beautiful prize I had gained. You've just confirmed that impression.'

With burning cheeks and downcast eyes, she said nothing. He took her chin, and raised her face to his.

'Look at me, Romy.'

She found herself glaring up at his face. It was lean, angular. Under the heavy brows, the wolf's eyes were almost shockingly beautiful in their intensity. They had an animal directness, a certainty that was underlined by the passionate, commanding slant of his mouth. 'I want to forget last night,' he said quietly. 'You were tired and overwrought, and I was unsympathetic. We were both to blame. Today we start afresh. Do you agree?'

'I don't want to be uncooperative.' She shrugged with little grace.

He touched her throat with appreciative fingers. 'Your blush is quite gorgeous. What on earth are you embarrassed about?'

She made no effort to hide the antipathy in her expression. 'Well, I'd rather you let me dress,' she replied shortly.

'I'm your husband,' he said, his fingers trailing downward. 'And you have no reason to be ashamed of your body. It is bewitchingly beautiful.'

'Then you had a rare treat just now,' she replied, hiding her embarrassment under sarcasm.

'I did,' he agreed equably. 'I could pose you nude on a pedestal, Romy, and look at you for hours.'

'You would soon grow bored!'

'I think not,' he replied in a velvety murmur. She tried to turn away as he bent to kiss her, but he tilted her face back, one hand cupping her chin. His mouth was warm and, as always, searching. And, as always, her own mouth responded with a tightening of its defences, a refusal to respond.

He took her in his arms, compelling her to accept his kiss. His strength was formidable. In his every movement, Romy felt that he was utterly sure of what he was doing, utterly indifferent to what she felt or thought. He made her feel helpless, almost irrelevant. She felt her senses swimming, starting to melt under the onslaught of his passion.

Was it passion? Or something much more calculating? Her body tautened as she grew aware of the feeling that she was being manipulated. Seduced by an expert, a man who had seduced a thousand women; seduced quite deliberately and coldly. She fought away from him, her breath coming quickly. 'No!'

Xavier's fingers bit into her arms. 'Always "no". Why?'

'Have a little respect for my wishes! This is hardly the place for an intimate chat,' she said stiffly. 'The maid is in the bedroom . . .'

'Not any more,' Xavier said with the ghost of a smile. 'I have sent her away. We are quite alone, Romy. And what better place for intimacy than this?'

But there was no warmth in his eyes, and the smile was as cool as a November morning. Romy knew that he was angry. Taking advantage of his feelings to avoid the uneasy situation, she turned away from him, and started brushing her hair in the mirror. 'I'm sorry about last night,' she said in a stilted voice. 'You're right—I *was* tired. I didn't intend to anger you like that. I was just rather emotional and upset.' She met his eyes in the glass briefly. 'And I don't insist that our relationship is hostile, as you said last night. I just want it to be free of pretence. I'm quite willing to start with a clean slate.'

He studied her reflection in silence for a moment, his eyes slightly narrowed. Then he smiled again, without making any comment on what she'd said.

'It's a little late for breakfast, and a little early for lunch. I have an American friend who eats what she calls "brunch" at this hour. Would you care to join me?'

'Yes, please.'

'Then I shall expect you downstairs in fifteen minutes,' he continued. 'Concetta will show you the way to the breakfast-room.'

She brushed her hair with regular, unthinking strokes after he'd left. The uneasy feeling remained that, far from patching anything up, that little encounter had just opened wider cracks in the delicate fabric of this marriage.

She hadn't meant to clash with Xavier this morning, and in this silent aftermath she was now regretting her sarcasm. She could have been a damned sight more conciliatory. Could have let him kiss her, and accepted his olive-branch with grace.

But there was something about him that made the blood

surge in her veins, obscuring her mind with a red mist. Perhaps it was the way his words cut her, or perhaps it was some deeper antipathy, some chemical aversion that she could do nothing about. She was afraid of him, yet she didn't have enough common sense to let that fear make her more reasonable!

'You must *try*,' she urged her reflection in a determined whisper. But her own eyes glared back at her, resentful and rebellious, contradicting the good intentions on her lips.

The 'brunch' was a full-scale meal. The grey-haired Sergio, whom she'd met last night, supervised a succession of beautifully prepared dishes. Romy guessed that all meals at Luca, no matter how impromptu, received the same kind of attention from the staff. Despite his dignity, she caught Sergio's friendly eye twinkling at her, as though it pleased him to see her fresh young face at the table.

They ate in an alcove by a window that looked out over an orchard of orange and lemon trees.

Xavier ate sparingly, despite the elaborate preparations, and Romy, if anything, ate even less. Xavier was in his most urbane and charming mood, as though nothing untoward had happened upstairs. With wit and humour, he explained the origins of the many exquisite furnishings in the room. She stared in awe at a beautiful painting of Venice that hung on the wall opposite, while he told her that it was a Canaletto, a superb piece that he had more than once thought of giving to a museum on permanent loan.

'It must cost a fortune to insure this house,' she said practically.

Xavier shrugged. 'I like to see my possessions around me. In some bank vault, they would be utterly wasted. The only thing better than this would be to make them public property, so that more people could enjoy them. Perhaps when I am a little older, I will make a gift of some of the more precious pieces to a gallery.'

Romy nodded. The gloomy impression of last night had given way to a better appreciation in the light of day. The *palazzo* was neither depressing nor decayed. On the contrary, there was wealth here, wealth of a sort unimaginable in England. Generations of de Lucas had exercised a flawless taste, adding to the impressive art collection that the house contained.

She'd come to the realisation that the house was itself a masterpiece of time, containing many diverse treasures of painting and furniture, of Persian carpets and Murano glass, of Greek marble and Roman bronze sculpture, of French needlework and Piedmontese tapestry.

Loving art as she did, this house was a magnificent place for her to live, and she knew that, though she could never love Xavier, she had fallen in love almost at once with his house!

'Have you telephoned your father yet?'

'N-no,' she said, starting as Xavier changed the subject.

'Why not?' He tossed his napkin down, a signal to the servants to clear the table. 'He will be wondering whether you've arrived safely. This is your house now,' he added. 'Everything here is yours to command. You should not feel shy to make your wishes known.'

'Then I'd like to telephone home now, if I may,' she said.

'Your home is here,' he reminded her quietly. He rose, and gestured towards the study. 'There is a telephone in there.'

She nodded her thanks, and went into the book-lined room. Sinking into a red leather armchair, she pulled the telephone over, and keyed in the number.

The sound of Papa's voice brought an instant lump to her throat, and it was an effort to sound relaxed and gay.

'The house is absolutely beautiful,' she enthused when she'd assured him she was fine, and that the trip hadn't been too tiring.

'I know,' he agreed. 'I was there many years ago, when Xavier's father was still alive. It's a wonderful place. I envy you your surroundings. Are you——?' He hesitated slightly. 'Are you and your husband at peace with one another?'

'No problems,' she said levelly. 'Don't worry about me, Papa.'

'I know you will be happy, Romy. Very happy. That means a lot to me. Xavier de Luca is a unique man, and he will make you the kind of husband most women only dream about. But you will also find that he is a man of strong will, and a man who must be treated with respect at all times.'

'I know,' she said in a low voice.

'Then I will say no more on the subject.'

'How's your health? Please tell me the truth.'

'My health is fine.' She could hear the smile in his voice. 'I've been for another check-up, and they say the signs are much better. Don't worry about me, darling. Or the business. Everything is beginning to sort itself out, though it will be a long road.'

'Just take care of yourself, Papa!'

'I will. You take care of yourself, too, my child. Please telephone again soon.'

'I will,' she promised, and after a few words of mutual affection she put the receiver down.

It was only then that she turned in the chair, and saw that Xavier was standing in the doorway, watching her, unmistakable irony in his eyes.

'Are you going to eavesdrop on all my conversations like that?' Romy demanded stiffly.

'Come, now; do we have secrets from one another?' He gave her a dry smile. 'The perfect wife has nothing to hide from her husband, surely?' He had stripped off his sweater, revealing a white silk shirt beneath it. One of the buttons at the midriff had come away, and he held it out to her now, with a threaded needle. 'The perfect wife should also take care of her husband's shirts. Could you sew this back on for me?'

'There are a dozen women in this house who could do that better than me,' she pointed out. But she took the needle, none the less, realising he was probably only trying to make her feel at home.

Xavier stood in front of her and, leaning forward in the chair, she began stitching the button back on. She could feel the hard muscles of his stomach under her fingers as she stitched.

His proximity was disturbing, and she avoided his eyes, concentrating on the simple task at hand.

'There is a great deal you have to learn about your new world,' he said, looking down at her. 'Not only about this house, but about the countryside you now live in. You will find life here quite different from England, and it would be well for you to understand the place you have to fill.'

'The place?'

'Within this society. To several hundred people, you are now the *baronessa*, and a person of far greater importance than any politician at Catania or Rome.'

'I don't understand that,' she said awkwardly.

'You will.' He considered her. 'I have made time in my schedule this afternoon to show you around the estate, and to give you some idea of its routines and traditions.'

'That will be most interesting,' she said levelly, irritated at his patronising tone. Her fingers brushed his skin as she made the final stitches. It was like warm velvet.

The button was on now, but she had no scissors to cut off the remaining thread. She bent forward without thinking to bite the cotton through. But, as her forehead brushed against his body, the intimacy of the gesture brought a sudden flush of blood to her face.

Hot with embarrassment, she cut the thread with sharp

teeth. The scent of his skin was in her nostrils as she drew quickly away. One glance at his face told her that Xavier, too, had felt that spark of awareness, and with scarlet cheeks Romy rose abruptly to her feet and put the needle on the desk.

'Thank you.'

She closed her eyes as she felt his palm touch her cheek, caressing her face with a tenderness she would not have believed him capable of. The shudder that spread across her skin raised goose-flesh in its wake. Feeling instinctively that he was about to kiss her, Romy pulled away in a spasm of panic.

His soft laughter made her curse herself for her stupidity.

'You are safe,' he assured her softly, 'for the time being. Come along, *Baronessa*. The guided tour of the establishment starts here.'

Four hours later, she had to admit that she was deeply impressed.

She'd been terrified of this tour, this presentation of her to Xavier's extended family.

But there had been nothing terrifying about it. The great estate ran like clockwork, and there was no doubt at all who that was due to. Xavier de Luca's administration was evidently efficient, humane and productive. The impression of thriving fields, lush vineyards and well-tended livestock was undeniably imposing. Luca was a life's work. It was easy to see that a set-up like this one could be the foundation for a very large fortune. Used as she was to seeing a large business run, she had to admit that this estate made Forlari Wines look like chicken-feed—and this was only the home-base of a much larger empire, extending across several countries.

But the estate of Luca was obviously the core of everything, and the centre of Xavier de Luca's world. He felt a profound love towards the estate, she knew that without having to be told. It was evident in every word he spoke about it.

Wherever they had gone, they had encountered nothing but smiling faces and warm welcomes from the workers and managers.

And she was beginning to understand what he had meant when he'd told her of the place she, too, had to fill within this society.

To say that it was run on feudal lines would be a distortion. This was a modern, highly organised estate, run by a large and dedicated workforce. Nevertheless, there was something very old-world in the way people treated her and Xavier. She knew instinctively that she was now an important personage in the lives of these strangers.

They looked up to her with almost the same expectations as they looked up to her husband: without humility—Sicilians were not very good on that—but with an automatic loyalty that somehow moved her very deeply. Some of the older generation had kissed her hand, while the younger ones had been more relaxed in their manners. But they had all looked at her in the same way: with respect, with affection, and with trust.

Almost casually, Xavier had been initiating her into the role she was to play, warning her of pitfalls she might meet, explaining the duties and obligations she would later have to face. This was a life very different from the hostessy, marquee-opening social round of an English knight's wife. She had found herself at the centre of a vital, living organisation which gave a home and a livelihood to more than two dozen large families. People were born on this estate, lived to be married on it, and to have families of their own. And to all of them she was now the *baronessa*, a figure who embodied protection and care.

Romy drew a deep breath as they got into the Range

Rover to drive back across the vineyards.

'Xavier, do you think I'm experienced enough to play the gracious lady to all these people?'

He glanced at her. 'What do you mean?'

'I feel so shy,' she said, her slender brows knitted in a frown. 'I don't know whether I can cope!'

'But you're charming,' he informed her with a smile. 'You've made them love you already.'

'Have I?' she doubted.

'Of course. You are young, beautiful, graceful and gentle. Everything they want their *baronessa* to be! It's all a state of mind, Romy. Just remember that although these people are strangers to you now, they are only waiting to help you and be your friends. They aren't looking to pick faults in you. Be confident, and you'll have no problems.'

'You make it sound so easy,' she sighed. 'You were born to this, remember? In any case, you're a man, and you're very different from me. You love organising this vast set-up, I can see that in every move you make. You're a born leader.'

'But that's my side of it. Your side is simply to be beautiful and loved.'

'Is that really all they want?'

He laughed softly. 'Oh, I think you can deliver what they're expecting.'

She looked at him sharply. 'You mean an heir for the estate?'

'That, too,' he agreed. 'But you undervalue yourself. You behaved with poise and charm. I thought you did splendidly this morning.'

Again, she stared at him in doubt. 'Really?'

Xavier smiled. 'Much better than I expected. You made me feel . . . very proud.'

She turned in the seat to look at his aquiline profile. 'That,' she said quietly, 'is the nicest thing you've ever said to me!'

He reached out, and laid his tanned hand on her thigh, sending butterflies through her stomach. 'If you were as adorable in our bedroom as you've been this morning in public, you would fill my heart with joy, Romy.'

She felt her face flood with hot colour. 'You mean, if I were to pretend to be eager and willing?'

'You wouldn't have to pretend for very long,' he purred. 'I assure you that you would soon be just as eager as I am!'

She veered away from the subject. 'Well,' she said, 'you've made me feel so much better. I was terrified about how this morning was going to turn out.'

Xavier took his hand away, looking amused. 'Were you so full of doubts, then?'

'I'm a London child, raised in the city. Country ways are very new to me. And . . . well, I think I'm just not arrogant enough for this kind of life.'

'What has arrogance got to do with it?' he enquired, quirking one eyebrow at her.

'You need arrogance in this line of business,' she informed him impudently. 'You, of all people, ought to understand that.'

'Thank you,' he said with a snort.

'And it's worse for a woman,' she assured him. 'A little pride gives you the confidence to impersonate the great lady, even if you weren't born to the part.' She paused. 'I imagine that your last wife played the role superbly.'

He glanced at her briefly. 'You sound very positive about that.'

'From what I remember of her,' Romy said with a touch of devilment, 'I think she was very suited to an aristocratic role. Are you saying she didn't do the lady of the manor to perfection?'

'Eva certainly brought an original touch to the role,' he agreed. 'But I have a feeling that you will be more loved than Eva ever was.'

'By whom?' she couldn't help asking.

'By all of them . . . all of us.' Before she could absorb that little hint, Xavier went on, 'which reminds me, your first big occasion as hostess is coming up soon.'

'What's that?' she asked.

'It's the *festa* of Santa Lucia next weekend.' Her unenlightened expression told him she didn't know what he was talking about. 'Saint Lucy's day,' he explained, 'the shortest day of the year. We always have a big party on that night, with a bonfire and dancing. And you, of course, will be the jewel in the crown.'

Romy stared at him. She'd noticed several men building a mountain of wood and dead branches in the garden, as though for a huge bonfire, but had thought nothing of it. 'Is that what they're doing with all that wood on the big lawn?'

'Yes. The fire has to be as big as possible, to make sure next summer is hot.' He shrugged at her incredulous face. 'Like most *festas*, it's a very old pagan ritual that goes way back before Christian times. Lighting a bonfire is a kind of fertility rite to chase away winter and fire up the sun again. It takes the grass a whole year to recover, but that's the price of tradition.' He smiled. 'It's a big occasion. You'll enjoy it. All the people you've met today will be there, not to mention another hundred or so assorted guests and neighbours. Everyone who can walk will come. The kitchen's already been busy for days, making *lasagne al forno* and half a dozen other traditional dishes, and they'll be roasting meat on the night as well.'

'And naturally,' Romy said uneasily, 'they'll all be very anxious to see their new *baronessa* dancing the light fantastic?'

'Exactly,' he confirmed. His grey eyes glanced at her face. 'Don't look so apprehensive. The idea is to have fun.'

'I can imagine.'

As they drove through the long lines of the vineyards, she

was brooding upon the things she'd learned today. Xavier was deeply respected here; but, more than that, he *belonged*. He fitted in here like the kingpin into a machine, the centre on which all the well-oiled wheels turned. It wasn't just tradition, either. He had expanded the estate enormously since his father's time, and had improved the quality of life of his employees beyond measure. He was an achiever, a doer.

Despite herself, she couldn't help a flicker of admiration for this powerful, effective man who was her husband. Ruthless and despotic he might be, but he was also a man who faced up to his responsibilities, and who held the fate of a great many people in his capable hands. That efficient side of his nature was something she hadn't considered before, perhaps because it only became evident here at Luca.

What he'd said to her this morning meant that she had a place, at his side. He'd said she'd made him proud of her, and that meant so much to her, more than she would ever admit to him. That, more than any amount of sarcasm, would make her try her level best to be a good wife to him.

Yet she could not bring herself to do more than respect Xavier. What was there about him that alienated her so?

And why did the thought of tonight bring such a contraction of fear to her stomach?

Sitting at her dressing-table at nine o'clock that night, Romy stared at her own reflection unseeingly. Her feelings were bruised, as though being with Xavier was a process of being consistently mauled. It was the smallest things he said and did that paradoxically hurt the most. The little put-downs, the patronising touches that galled her pride.

Why did his words hurt her so much? He knew just where she was most tender, most vulnerable. Damn him!

Did he mean to be funny when he slighted her? Or deliberately hurtful? The latter, almost certainly. He was the kind of man who enjoyed unsheathing his claws now and then. Not all the time. Just when he felt the need to inflict a little wanton pain.

Tonight over dinner, for example, he had been charming. But then, there had been an audience—the local doctor and his wife, who had dropped in for a drink, and stayed to supper.

The evening had been gay. Even Romy herself had thawed, and found herself smiling and laughing. Antagonistic as she felt towards her husband, she had to admit that he was socially gifted to an unusual extent. He had a potent charm that came without effort, as easy as turning on a tap.

And, no doubt, that turned off as easily.

Buoyed by his support, she was able to play his game for a few hours, and keep the mask in place, but the strain had started killing her enjoyment. Pleading tiredness, she had excused herself early, and had come up to the bedroom while Xavier concluded the evening.

She had undressed, washed briefly, and then, clad in her silk gown, had taken her make-up off, not caring whether that suited him or not. Why go through the hypocrisy of dolling herself up?

Xavier would not be long. The little doctor, she imagined, would consider it tactless in the extreme to keep Xavier from his new bride, and very soon her husband would be coming through the bedroom door . . .

She felt a cold chill spreading through her stomach. There could be no evasion tonight, no excuses. Tonight she was his, every inch of her, bought and paid for.

Her eyes focused on her reflection. This woman in the mirror was beautiful. In the past few months, her beauty had deepened, gained a luminous maturity. Whatever his feelings about Eva, he could never say that she was more beautiful. There, at least, she was a match for the last baroness. The face in the mirror was lovely, deep blue eyes and dark red lips set off by hair that was almost too black to be real. Even without make-up, even tired and tense-looking, she had a beauty that was dramatic, remarkable. Without vanity, she could think that Xavier de Luca had bought a bargain.

How would he take her tonight? With kisses and whispers? With the merciless efficiency of an animal mating?

For a moment she could almost feel that hard, naked body against hers, feel her woman's flesh yielding to his assault. A hot flush rose to her face, and she slammed the door of her mind shut on the image.

She rose from the stool, belting her gown around her tightly. Her breasts made soft peaks against the shimmering material. She was aware of a trembling in her legs, a sense of apprehension that was making her stomach ache. The waiting was the worst part.

She walked across the room to the little lacquered cabinet that she knew contained drinks and glasses. She'd been abstemious over supper, no more than a glass or two of white wine. She should have had more.

Romy sorted briefly through the bottles, and settled on the French brandy. It wasn't her usual drink; in fact, she would normally not have thought of it. But right now she felt urgently in need of the support strong drink could give her. If she were to face Xavier in bed tonight, she needed some kind of cushion for her sensibilities.

She poured a large measure into a brandy glass, and gulped at it determinedly. She was not too sophisticated to choke on the liquid fire, and it brought the tears to her eyes. She had to will herself to drain the glass.

She stood gasping for a moment, feeling the heat of the brandy flood her stomach, spreading into her veins. Then she poured herself a smaller measure, and walked to the window, glass in hand. The cognac was already starting to ease her tensed muscles.

Well, Papa and the business were safe now. But from here on she had to start paying the price! Martyrdom was nice in theory. In reality, it was very different. Facing a life with Xavier de Luca had been bearable while she'd been able to keep it all abstract. Facing it in practice might not be, not in any sense. In those dark days it had all seemed so logical, such a clever solution. She'd thought of nothing else but the pressure of her family's need, the urgency of saving Papa from a heart attack.

And now it was done. And she was left with only debts to pay, and no credits to cash in.

Her glass was empty. She walked back to the cabinet, feeling the blood pounding in her ears, and poured herself a third, more generous tot of cognac. The taste of it was sickening, but the effect wasn't bad. It numbed the brain, at least, and warmed the blood.

Knowing she wasn't finished with the bottle, she took it, and her glass, and curled up against the pillows on the bed.

What a situation! How had her life, so full of hope and promise a few short months ago, got itself into this tangle?

First Paul Mortimer, and what he'd done to her. Then the shock of Papa's financial disaster. And now, to cap it all, *this*.

The cognac burned a fiery track down her throat, dulling her emotions. She refilled her glass again, then again, her thoughts turning in slow, endless circles.

The fault was hers. Hers alone. Too much of a fool to tell that Paul was a rotter. Too soft to resist her family's pressure to wed a man she disliked. Too awkward to be complaisant to the husband she was now wedded to. When are you going to grow up? she asked herself savagely.

Xavier came in, his eyes widening as they took in the bottle in her hand. 'What on earth are you doing?'

'Having a drink.' She sat up to face him, a lock of hair

dropping in front of her eyes. 'And having a little heart-to-heart with myself, too. Want a drink?'

He glanced at the level of the cognac, eyes cool and grey. 'You've had far too much.'

'Have I?' Amused at his expression, she smiled. 'I was making my way right down to the bottom, as a matter of fact.'

'Is this your idea of a joke?'

'No joke. Call it thera-therapeu——' She gave up on the word. 'Call it medicine.'

'I might have known,' he said icily, 'when you left the table early. I might have known you had something like this planned.'

'I did *not* plan it.' She sat up straighter. Her gown had slipped, revealing the creamy curve of one breast for a moment. She pulled it straight, and glared at him through tumbled hair. 'You've been with that boring little doctor far too long, leaving me up here alone. I just wanted a little drink to help me face . . .'

'To help you face my lovemaking?' he prompted as she tailed off.

Romy shrugged, turning away. 'You said it, not me. Sorry I'm not adorable, the way you want me to be. But what the hell? I'm ready for my lord and master now.'

'Don't talk like a slut,' he snapped. 'It doesn't suit you.'

'How the hell do *you* know what suits me and what doesn't?' she demanded insolently. 'You don't know the first damned thing about me. I sometimes wonder what you married me for.' She swept the dark hair away from her face to glare up at him. 'Anyway, you've paid for the merchandise, so why don't we just get on with it?'

She was starting to shrug off her gown when she felt his fingers bite into her bare shoulders. She gasped in pain as he swung her round to face him.

'Don't try my patience much more, Romy.' His voice

carried ice, like an arctic wind. 'I have allowed you a great deal of leeway so far, out of consideration for your age and immaturity. But jokes like this will wear very thin if you attempt to repeat them. You understand me?'

She met Xavier's eyes, steel-grey, like a wolf's, and felt anger start to break through the muzzy wall of the cognac. The alcohol had given her courage to face up to him. 'I'm not your slave, whatever you may have paid for me!'

'And I am not your fool,' he retorted. 'Don't treat me like one.'

'You're hurting me!' The upper curves of her breasts were uncovered, but he did not look at them. In her present mood, his indifference to her femininity infuriated her. 'If you want to make love to me, then go ahead, and welcome. Just get it over with. If not, give me the brandy back, and I'll amuse myself for the rest of the evening!'

'I warned you once before to cultivate a little grace,' he said in a rasping voice. 'These melodramatic displays don't impress me in the slightest.'

'Don't they?' Her eyes blazed blue. 'I'm just trying to give value for money, dear husband. I've been sitting here thinking about how it feels to be a bought woman. Perhaps I should have been wondering how it feels to be the sort of man who has to buy his wives!'

Xavier's face tightened. 'Cognac disagrees with your temper, I see,' he said coolly. 'Your choice of language is not pretty, Romy.'

'Ah. You don't like the truth. I forgot.'

The authority in his face was emphasised by the severe lines around his mouth and eyes. 'You are my wife. And nothing will change that.'

'Your devotion to the institution of marriage is most touching, for someone who's already had one divorce,' Romy sneered. 'I wonder why. Is it nostalgia? Or the piety of the lapsed Christian? This marriage is meaningless, as you well know.'

'It has exactly the same meaning as all other marriages,' Xavier retorted. 'No more, no less.'

Her laugh was jagged. 'Who are you trying to kid?' She sat back against the pillows, and stared back at him with eyes that were bright with cognac. 'Do you really imagine that this can last? I have no such illusions, Xavier. We have nothing in common. *Nothing*. We detest each other. We'll be filing for divorce within a year, you know that as well as I do!'

'I know nothing of the sort,' he said grimly.

'No?' she said. 'For such an intelligent man, you have a remarkable capacity for self-deception, Xavier. The truth is that this relationship can't possibly last.'

He put the cognac bottle down on to the bedside-table. 'Whether the relationship lasts or not,' he said ruthlessly, 'I assure you that the marriage will last.'

'Not if I don't want it to,' Romy snapped. 'I could get a divorce tomorrow if I wanted!'

Xavier's mouth moved in a smile that was wickedly mocking. 'I will never let you go. Hate me or love me, you belong to me, Roma.' His eyes locked on hers with fierce meaning. 'You belong to me.'

He turned and walked to the door. 'Where are you going?' she called shakily.

He didn't look back. 'I will sleep elsewhere. There's plenty more cognac in the bottle. Drink the lot. Amuse yourself.'

'Damn you!' she yelled after him. 'I'll never give in to you! You hear me? I'll never——'

But she was shouting at a closed door. Romy felt herself dissolve into racking sobs, against her will.

The reality of what she'd done had only started to come home to her. One look into those ice-coloured wolf's eyes was enough to tell her that he meant what he said. There *was* no escape. He would never permit her to leave him.

CHAPTER FIVE

ROMY heard Xavier's Range Rover coming up the drive towards the house.

Romy murmured her thanks to the old gardener who had been explaining the Sicilian names of the plants to her, and turned to watch her husband arrive. She was feeling frail this morning, very frail indeed. She'd awoken alone, with a splitting head, and her cheeks stained with last night's tears.

It had taken a long, long time to get her act together. After a glass of orange juice and three aspirins, she had been exploring the beautiful garden, taking a kind of perverse satisfaction in the winter cold that bit into her body, her thoughts as bleak as the November sky above.

She hadn't been so tipsy that she was unaware of the damage she'd done last night. How sluttish she must have seemed to him, how disgusting. Such a long way from the icy dignity she'd planned to show him. That was the way to handle Xavier. Behave like a woman made of marble, cold and haughty. Show him that she was no silly girl, but a mature and adult woman.

Xavier parked the big car, and walked up to meet her, three spaniels following eagerly at the heels of his supple leather boots. As Xavier approached, she hugged the fluffy mohair jersey around her shoulders, shivering slightly. Let him not be too harsh, she prayed inwardly. The way she felt right now, one cruel word would make her cry.

He stopped in front of her. The rough Shetland sweater he wore emphasised the rocky breadth of his chest and shoulders, and the faded whipcord jeans hugged the muscles of long legs that stood slightly apart, almost in the aggressive poise of a fencer.

Indeed, there was something like duellists in the way they faced each other, as though the memory of last night was a tangible presence between them.

Romy felt her heartstrings tighten painfully. He looked different in the country clothes, more natural, and yet somehow even more sexually male. Not that there was any mistaking him for a peasant; even if you hadn't noticed that the exquisite boots were handmade, or hadn't caught the gleam of a heavy gold watch at his wrist, every inch of his frame spoke of arrogant power.

And the face was of a man used to command and conquer, a man capable of powerful emotions and unyielding will.

They stared at each other for a short while, the tension so tangible that one of the spaniels began to whimper, and pawed uneasily at its master's leg. Then the wind whipped a cloud of Romy's newly washed black hair across her eyes, and as though the moment were broken she stooped to pat the dogs. They crowded to her stroking hands, the warm, licking tongues eager to greet her.

She felt his fingers bite into her arm, his strength hauling her effortlessly back to her feet. Fierce eyes glittered at her. 'Don't greet the dogs before you greet me.'

Any conciliatory thoughts vanished. 'Oh, dear,' she said acidly. 'Am I forgetting my place again? I should have kissed your hand, I'm sorry. Or should I have kissed your boots?'

'A simple word would have done,' he growled, releasing her. 'Does it give you some kind of pleasure to stand out here alone, in the freezing cold?'

'Yes,' she said shortly, 'it gives me a kind of pleasure.'

'I must be sure to have the cooks keep plenty of wormwood and gall in stock, then. For your special treats.'

'How amusing,' she said coldly. 'In any case, I have not

been alone. The gardener has been explaining the names of the flowers to me.'

Xavier glanced at the stooped old man who was busying himself with a vine some distance away. 'Wonderful company for a young bride,' he commented disdainfully.

'You hold a great many people in contempt, don't you?' Romy said shortly. 'You're too used to commanding and being obeyed, *signore*.'

'Is that bad?' he enquired, his eyes meeting hers.

'As I told you before,' she informed him deliberately, 'arrogance is necessary to a man in your position. Unfortunately, it's hardly an attractive quality in normal life.'

He smiled without humour, and took her arm. 'And as I once told you, our lives are not normal. How do you feel this morning?' he asked as they walked to the house.

'Rough,' she said succinctly. 'I presume you're going to read me the riot act?'

'Judging by your face, that won't be necessary. Do you know how much cognac you drank last night?'

'I'm not used to strong drink.'

'That much is obvious.' He gave her a dry look. 'Who do you think put you to bed?'

'Oh.' The picture was hardly a glamorous one, and she shut it away hastily. 'I think that's the first time in my life I've ever drunk too much. I don't want you to think that I'm eager to repeat the experience. Or that I make a habit of it.'

'I'm glad to hear that,' he said without apparent irony. 'Shall we forget the whole incident? Let's go and eat.'

The lunch was hot, but the mood wasn't. If she'd wanted to cripple their relationship last night, she could hardly have found a better way of doing it. Xavier's manner towards her was cool and formal, and their talk was stilted. He was an expert, she knew, at making her feel uncomfortable; yet that didn't make the effect on her any the less crushing.

'After lunch,' he announced, 'I want to introduce you formally to the household staff. It's time you met them all, and learned their names.'

'Very well,' Romy said quietly. As soon as the meal was over, he carried out his intention, the staff filing in, wearing the various uniforms of their trades and duties. They looked as shy as she felt, but not unfriendly.

Some, like Concetta and Sergio, the major-domo, she already knew. She made a determined effort to connect the others with the names she now learned—Tomas, Lucia, Alva, Vito, Mauro. She shook hands with each in turn, repeating their names as Sergio explained the duties of each, and giving each a smile and a special word. She wanted them to like her and trust her, and she had enough experience to know that unless she established good relations with her staff she would never have a well-run household.

She was conscious of Xavier following her with intent eyes, his arms folded as he leaned against the table to watch.

At the end of the line, Sergio turned to her. 'On behalf of all of us,' he said with a smile, 'welcome to your home, *Baronessa*.' He spoke a few more words of welcome, and concluded by giving her a slight bow. 'We are all honoured to have you among us, and we want you to feel that you may rely on us completely.'

'You've all been very kind to me,' Romy replied, glancing from face to face. 'I want to thank you for that. It means a great deal to me to feel that I have so many friends here. I would like to be your friend, too, and I hope you will come to me, any of you, if there is anything you need, or any problem you have.'

Quick smiles appeared on all the faces, and then the impromptu meeting broke up.

Xavier was watching her with smoky eyes. 'You amaze me,' he said quietly, when they were alone.

'Why?' she asked.

'Sometimes you are so poised and gracious. Like now. You make me feel that I've made the best marriage a man ever made. You make me feel like the proudest husband in Sicily. And then, when we are alone, you behave with all the devilment and vices of an unbroken mare!'

'Perhaps,' she said, flushing at his praise, 'that's to do with some effect you have on me, Xavier.'

He raised one ironic eyebrow. 'I wish I knew how to undo that effect. We have the afternoon free. Would you like me to show you round the house?'

'I'd love that.' She smiled. 'I've been longing to see it all.'

'Then come.'

The two hours that followed were among the happiest and closest they'd yet spent together. Her love of art and history had made the house fascinating and wonderful to her from the start, and she was able to appreciate the depth of knowledge which Xavier had about his possessions. He had dates and names at his fingertips, knowing the history and provenance of all the sculptures and paintings and gleaming pieces of superlative furniture.

'You have wonderful things,' she sighed at one point, overwhelmed by the magnificence of it all.

'*We* have wonderful things,' he corrected. 'These things are yours as well as mine.' The dark eyes met hers. 'Everything here is yours, you must understand that. You are the mistress here, and you must make any changes, any additions, that you want to.'

In one of the upstairs salons, a beautiful room with its own vast terrace, she turned, and suddenly saw the portrait.

The painting was centred on the main wall, flanked by two ornate marble tables bearing exquisite Chinese vases, an arrangement that gave it an unmistakable sense of importance.

Not that the painting needed any kind of enhancement. The woman who was the subject was beautiful, and the imperious way she stared out of the canvas was very striking.

Romy stared back at the green eyes, noting the rather wide, imperious mouth, the high cheekbones, the masses of platinum-blonde hair.

'Eva,' she said, her voice suddenly flat.

'Yes.' Xavier nodded, coming to stand beside her. 'My last baroness, so to speak. You like the portrait?'

'It's very like her,' Romy replied. 'And it's a fine work. It has impact.' She studied the painting with narrowed eyes. Beautifully dressed and beautifully presented as she was, the woman in the portrait did not generate any warmth. The impression she gave was rather of coldness and haughtiness. The kind of bitchiness that would be an irresistible turn-on for some men. 'You must miss her,' she said shortly.

'What makes you say that?'

'You wouldn't keep her portrait hanging here otherwise.' She gave him a searching glance. 'It's hardly usual for divorced couples to cherish paintings of one another, is it?'

'I do not know,' Xavier replied easily. 'I keep the picture for three reasons. One of them is that it really is rather a good piece, irrespective of the subject matter. It was done by Angelucci, and his work sells for a lot of money these days.' He smiled slightly at the woman in the painting. 'For another reason, the painting goes with this room. This was always Eva's room. She furnished it, and she spent a lot of time here.'

'I see,' Romy said flatly, making a mental resolution never to come in here again if she could help it. How many other places in this house were 'Eva's'? she wondered acidly. How many more times was she going to have to come across the presence of her predecessor? She folded her arms. 'What is the third reason you have for keeping it?'

'Ah.' His smile was smooth. 'The third reason is the most banal: for old times' sake.'

'I see,' Romy said again, her voice thin.

'I am not the sort of man to cast off old friends,' he went on, apparently unaware of Romy's rising temper. 'What does the Bible say? "Forsake not an old friend; for the new is not comparable to her; a new friend is as new wine; when it is old thou shalt drink it with pleasure."' He changed the gender in the quotation but its meaning was clear.

'How true,' Romy gritted. That had been aimed straight at her heart, and it had hurt like hell. Damn him and his quotations! After the closeness they'd just shared, how could he wound her like this? 'I hadn't quite seen you as a Bible reader, *signore*. But I was forgetting—even the Devil can quote Scripture.'

Xavier shrugged. The flush on Romy's cheekbones betrayed her sparkling anger. But his eyes were amused, as though he were intensely enjoying her feelings. 'I have a retentive memory for some things,' he replied.

'So it seems.' She gave him a bright smile. 'Especially for women, I take it?'

'There are some women who leave an indelible impression on the memory.'

'Like Eva?'

He glanced down at her, but did not reply. Romy glanced around the room. 'If this is an example of her style, I'm impressed. She has taste.'

'Yes,' he agreed. 'She has an instinctive grace, an ability to cope.'

'How nice,' Romy said frostily. 'You must miss such talent around you.'

Xavier's eyes glittered. 'I feel sure you will learn—given time.'

'Kind of you to say so.'

'Not at all.' He took her arms, as urbane as though he hadn't noticed how tense her muscles were. 'You still have not answered my question. Do you like the painting?'

'I have no feelings about it one way or the other,' she

answered, lifting her chin slightly.

'Are you sure?' he asked, smiling grey eyes probing hers. 'You've shown very fine taste in art so far this afternoon. It's not like you to be so neutral about a painting. If you have the slightest objection, my dear, I will have it removed this very afternoon.'

'I wouldn't dream of that,' she assured him. If this game of cat and mouse amused him, then let him get his money's worth, she decided. 'As you say, the painting is a fine one. Why remove it from a room which was so obviously designed around it?'

'Such magnanimity,' he purred, 'deserves to be rewarded. We must see whether we can prevail upon Angelucci to paint your picture, too.'

'Oh, I wouldn't dream of that, either,' Romy said disdainfully. 'Such extravagance hardly suits the humble subject matter.' She disengaged her arm from his, and walked deliberately away from the portrait. 'You were telling me about this walnut console,' she said in a clear voice. 'Venetian, early eighteenth century, wasn't it?'

There were no guests that night. No cognac, no loneliness, no excuse to put off their lovemaking.

They stood facing one another in the crimson bedroom. As an actress on a stage where she had once experienced a crushing failure, Romy felt her poise falter and flutter. A kind of sweet terror had her in its grip, paralysing her. Her heart was thudding, an uneven, rapid pulse against her ribs.

He was magnificently beautiful, and suddenly she knew she wanted him.

'Well?' he asked softly. 'Are we going to make love, Romy? Or must I take you by force?'

For answer, she raised her face to his, her lips already parted as his mouth claimed hers. His tongue was a sweet invasion, demanding and hungry, and his arms held her so tightly that she was almost breathless.

Heat saturated her, as though the sun had suddenly shone into her soul through a flung-open gateway. The warmth of being wanted by him reached deep into her soul, driving out all doubts. He encompassed her, more potent and important than anything else in her life.

Her head was swimming, the world about them seeming to vanish, her body seeming to melt into something light and floating in his arms.

Nothing had any substance any more, nothing except their caressing mouths, and the exhilarating closeness of their embrace. As their kiss deepened, Xavier's hand possessively cupped the yielding sweetness of her breast. His potency was overwhelming. The shoulders she clung to were solid with muscle and, as she pressed close to him, the hardness at his loins told her he was erect. With the dreamy eroticism of a cat, she pressed her belly against his desire, and heard the husky moan of pleasure rumble in his throat.

Xavier unfastened her clothes with sure fingers, until she stood, clad only in the lacy triangle of her pants, before him.

'You're so beautiful,' he whispered, almost in awe. 'You make my heart ache.'

Taking her by the hand, he led her to the bed and laid her down against the dusky vermilion sheets. Her body was pale as ivory in the soft light, her breasts rising and falling to her rapid breathing.

He kissed her lips tenderly, as though sensing her tension.

'Don't be afraid,' he said softly. 'I want to give you only pleasure.' His hands were gentle as they caressed her body, but the hunger in his eyes as they devoured her body made her tremble.

He rose to take his own clothes off. She watched him undress through half-closed eyelashes. He was beautiful, majestic. His man's body was tanned, etched with muscles that rippled and tightened as he moved. So different from her; he was as tanned as she was pale, his potency counterpointing her femininity with mysterious perfection. He stripped to his black briefs, and turned for a moment to unfasten the gold chain he wore round his neck.

Romy knew she would never forget this moment. Watching the rugged muscles of his back in the golden light, she knew she would never know a man like this again.

Then he stripped off his briefs, allowing her a glimpse of his nakedness as he came to her, his eyes smiling, reaching for her. His skin was warm under her palms, the firm muscles dense and tight with anticipation.

She hid her face against Xavier's shoulder, stifling her own moan of pleasure as his hands caressed her breasts, brushing the swollen nipples, moving downwards to her loins, finding the melting response of her womanhood.

His caress was expert, exquisite, his fingers understanding everything about her, knowing her every secret wish. He made her cry out loud with desire, her body pressing to his.

'I want you,' he whispered roughly, his magnificent face flushed with desire. 'I want you *now* . . .'

'Yes,' she whispered raggedly, 'don't make me wait, my love . . .'

He moved on to her, his weight a delicious burden. Her thighs parted to admit his hips, her mouth opening under his kiss.

Then her body drew into a taut arc under his, as his manhood filled her, deep and potent and overwhelmingly sexual.

He made love with an intensity she'd never dreamed of, as though he wanted to touch her very soul with his. She could feel his hard, lean thighs thrusting against her, his arms crushing her. Passion was unfolding in her like an exotic flower, its petals brushing against the erotic zones of her body. Romy felt an achingly sweet, feminine response start to flow in her blood like warm honey.

There could be no comparison between this man and Paul Mortimer. Paul's lovemaking had been like a pale candle to the searing sun of what she instantly felt with Xavier.

Could he guess that? Did he feel jealousy about Paul, the way she was wounded by her own thoughts of Eva? Did he ever think of Paul possessing her, using her body for his pleasure?

The thought of Paul made her falter for a moment, distracting her from her pleasure.

Sensing that, Xavier bent to kiss her. She turned her mouth away, whimpering, but his response was to knot his fingers in her black hair, forcing her lips to his. For a quivering moment she resisted, but then she opened her mouth to gasp.

He kissed her parted lips, his own mouth fierce and hungry. For a wild moment, their kiss was a scalding contact within the torrent of their lovemaking, his tongue exploring the secret depths of her mouth with the commanding assurance of a master.

His resolution was so much stronger than hers. He was thrusting this delicious pleasure on her whether she wanted it or not, his body allowing no argument. With utter confidence, Xavier was guiding her to a peak that was almost unbearable, almost ready to explode, prolonging the exquisite agony until she thought she could bear it no longer.

There were no more thoughts, not of Paul, not of anything. Only Xavier mattered. She could not stop herself from crying out at last, her voice broken and husky. Tension drained out of her in the long shudder of bliss. Then her strained muscles crumpled, and Xavier slid down beside her, releasing her. The intensity of the experience had left her shaking, dazed, and her eyes were swimming with tears.

It had happened at last. She was his. And, as though some great bridge had been crossed, she felt that there could never be any going back, not ever again.

She took a long, shaky breath, the salt tears brimming over her shut lids and spilling down her cheeks. Xavier looked down at her, saying nothing. She covered her face with her hands, wiping away her tears. For a few moments he let her cry. Then he took her arms, more gently this time, and kissed her mouth lightly.

'I was too rough with you.'

'You weren't.' She tried to wrest control of her ragged emotions as she pulled the tumbled sheets up around herself. Her limbs were trembling, and her skin was flushed. They lay in silence for a long while, while their breathing returned to something like normal. The softly lit bedroom was warm and intimate, and outwardly the picture was one of a flawlessly happy marriage, of two beautiful people side by side after love.

The reality was very different. Lying beside him, Romy willed the soft and tender feelings in her to subside. Why should she accept that the act they'd just completed had brought them any closer together, or had changed anything between them? The ecstasy he had given her was a purely physical thing, and she was fully aware of the perils of letting it interfere with her emotions. It was something that must not be yielded to.

After a while, Xavier rose, and went to the cabinet to pour them both a drink. Romy watched him from under covert lashes. His body was splendid, deeply bronzed and stunningly male. The lamplight on his skin made it glow with power. He was hard with muscle across the chest and shoulders, yet so lean that his ribs were tightly outlined, and the muscles of his stomach were quartered in clear relief under the curling black hair. His legs were lean and athletic, and when he moved it was like watching a panther, or some big hunting cat, all lithe instincts and springlike expectancy.

He came back to bed with two small glasses of Cointreau. She sipped the potent liqueur, enjoying the orange-skin sharpness that overlaid the alcohol. It was just what she felt like.

'You hardly said a word or made a sound.' He was watching her with smoky eyes. 'I've never made love to a more silent woman. Why do you hold so much back from me, Romy?'

'Perhaps there's nothing there to give,' she said, in an attempt at defiance.

'Anything is more than nothing,' he said. 'And you gave nothing just now. After today, I had the idea we'd drawn closer.'

'I'll try and be more vocal next time.' The irony was wasted on him. He leaned on one elbow, watching her face with those damnably penetrating grey eyes. In the secluded afterglow of lovemaking, she felt very vulnerable to him.

'Tell me something. And tell me the truth. Do you still love this Paul Mortimer—the one who let you down?'

So he *had* let thoughts of Paul enter his mind. 'Of course not.'

'Why "of course not"? You once told me you'd learned a great deal about human relationships from him. You also said you didn't intend to let another man take advantage of you. That indicates you felt pretty deeply about him.'

'I did once,' she confirmed. 'I thought I loved Paul. He was different from anyone I'd met before. He was——' She shrugged awkwardly. 'But you don't want to hear all this drivel . . .'

'I don't have anything pressing to do right now,' he pointed out, stretching his beautiful body out beside her. 'How was he different?'

'Oh, he seemed very special to me. Intelligent, sensitive, creative . . . but it was all a fraud. A front. There was no depth to him, no giving, only taking. Even before I discovered that he was married, I think I had unconsciously realised what a mistake I'd made with him. He was an emotionally inadequate man, the sort of man who preys on women without even knowing that he's a predator.' She rolled over to put her glass down. 'You said you'd met him before we got married. Where was that?'

'I asked him to meet me for a drink.' Xavier's handsome face was expressionless. 'He came to the Athenaeum. We talked for an hour.'

She shook her head. 'What made you want to meet him? Morbid curiosity?'

'Perhaps. But I had other reasons. I felt he could give me some extra information about you.'

'You're a very thorough man,' Romy said drily. 'No wonder your investments are so sound. I take it you weren't too impressed with Paul?'

Xavier's lip curled. 'He didn't strike me as the stuff of a maiden's romantic dreams. I found him shallow and trivial. I was glad to see the back of him.'

Romy drew the sheets around her naked breasts, aware of a throbbing ache in her loins. His lovemaking had not been so much rough as very thorough, and very deep. If he was intent on giving her a child, he was certainly going the right way about it. 'In which case, why do you ask whether I still love him?'

'To try and explain your behaviour,' he said calmly. 'You told me you hated me last night, and I wonder why that should be.'

'Given the circumstances of my marriage,' Romy said warily, 'is there any reason you can think of why I should bear you any love? But I was angry then. And I'd had far too much to drink. I don't hate you, and I regret saying that.'

'Yet you go out of your way to hurt me,' he said coolly.

'Hurt you?' Romy smiled. 'You are impervious to hurt, Xavier. Impervious to anything *I* could do to try and hurt you, anyway. We made a bargain. A deal. You married me because you wanted heirs, and because you thought you could get a share in Forlari Wines. And I married you to save my father from disgrace and disaster.'

'Can you really talk about deals and bargains,' he asked contemptuously, 'at a time like this?'

'What better time?' Romy retorted.

'You puzzle me,' he said drily, looking at her with keen grey eyes. 'You seemed to have no objection to making love a few moments ago. Yet when we discuss your emotions, you want me to believe you have none. That's hardly womanly. Are the two things unconnected in your mind?'

She looked at him from under a tumbled fringe of raven hair. 'I can't speak for other women. They are in my case.'

'I see. In that case, we're wasting our time talking, aren't we?' He drained his glass, and reached for her, his eyes wickedly intent. 'Why don't we keep this strictly physical? Let's repeat the performance—and see whether we can rouse a sound out of you this time.'

What had passed between them in the night left no warmer feelings in its wake the next morning.

If anything, Romy felt that she had never been more unhappy in his company. Over the breakfast-table, she could hardly meet his eyes, her replies to his easy questions monosyllabic and terse.

The memory of that heat and passion in their bed was like a barrier in front of her. It humiliated her to remember how he had dominated her senses, and how easily her husband's lovemaking had conquered her will to resist.

Of course, she reflected sourly, he was an acknowledged expert at seduction. She was merely the latest in a very long line, and getting the benefit of a lot of experience . . .

'Oh,' he said casually, looking up from his newspaper, 'I almost forgot to tell you. Eva rang this morning, while you were still asleep. She will be here this afternoon.'

'*Eva?*' Romy sat up, putting down her spoon. 'What's she coming for?' she demanded tightly.

'A social call, very little more.'

'"Very little more"?' she repeated. 'What does that mean?'

'Eva and I still have various things in common. There are things we need to discuss.' He considered the newspaper, without elaborating on that. 'You've met her before, of course.'

'Yes. Under rather different circumstances.' Anger was prickling through her. So, she had been right. Eva was coming to inspect the new arrival! 'You might have consulted me before inviting her,' she gritted out.

'Unfortunately, you were fast asleep,' he smiled easily, pouring her more orange juice. 'It seemed a shame to wake you.'

'Oh, did it?' A servant was clearing away the used plates, and she suspended her words for a while, fuming with impatience. He gave her a quizzical glance when they were alone. 'You seem upset.'

'Of course I'm upset!' Romy said, her voice lifting. 'Are you deliberately trying to humiliate me?'

'My dear child, I thought you might be glad of the opportunity to glean some hints from my ex-wife,' he drawled. 'You were telling me how much you needed to learn.'

'You——' She was lost for words. 'We haven't even been married a week!'

'Ah.' He looked as though he had just got the point of a rather obscure joke. 'You are jealous. But I thought you felt nothing for me?' he enquired silkily.

'It's not a question of my feelings for you,' she snapped. 'It's a matter of my position here in your household! You keep telling me about the exalted role you expect me to play, and now you do this. You're putting me in a very awkward situation, Xavier. Why not invite half a dozen of your former lovers, while you're about it? You could start a harem!'

'The idea is interesting, but unfeasible,' he purred. 'I assure you, Eva is dying to meet you. And if you do not get on——' He waved his glass at the room. 'This house is big enough to accommodate you and her without friction for one afternoon.'

'There is no house big enough to accommodate two wives,' Romy said shortly.

Xavier's expression was unchanged. He was a stunningly handsome figure. Handsome in the way only very heartless men could be. 'I hardly agree with you, my love. You are over-reacting to an absurd degree. Sure you won't have some more orange juice? It's freshly squeezed, and full of vitamins.'

Eva von Schimmel arrived at two o'clock, in a yellow Ferrari, wearing a leopard-skin coat over a Dior dress that matched the Ferrari's yellow.

Real leopard skin, of course. Eva was not the sort of woman to have much concern for the welfare of protected species.

Romy, waiting tautly in the salon, smiled without humour. She'd instinctively known that Eva's arrival would be spectacular. Her own outfit, a dark grey suit with a wide leather belt and a loose jacket, had been chosen for its restrained elegance. She only hoped that, confronted with leopard skin and firefly yellow, she would not simply vanish into the background.

She watched Eva greeting Xavier through the window. It was a tender scene. The spotted arms that wrapped themselves round Xavier's neck were avid, and the mouth-to-mouth kiss went on a long time.

Then, arm in arm with her, Xavier led his ex-wife into the

house.

'It's so *good* to be back!'

Pulling off her driving gloves, and tossing them down on to a table, Eva extended long, slender fingers to Romy, who took them with as much cool grace as she could muster. The other woman leaned forward to give her a continental-style double kiss, among a cloud of Joy; but no contact took place, the 'kisses' being merely pretty noises two inches away from each cheek.

Green eyes raked over her briefly. 'But she's *exquisite*, darling!' Eva turned to give Xavier an admiring smile, as though complimenting him on the purchase of a fine piece of Dresden. 'Truly exquisite. How have you managed to be so clever?'

'You forget. I am always clever.' He smiled with no show of tension. 'Romy, I would like you to meet Eva von Schimmel, my first wife.'

'How do you do?' Romy said formally, and for a brief moment the two women sized one another up. Romy's dislike was as instantaneous as a flame igniting. Eva was, as she had remembered, both tall and slender. And, although there was an age difference of at least five years between them, Eva had the smooth, glowing skin and lithe limbs of a tennis star. The platinum-blonde hair was flawlessly arranged to frame a wide, slightly catlike face, with emerald eyes, a wide mouth, and porcelain-white teeth.

'You were just a *child* when I last saw you.' Eva spoke perfect, slightly accented English. Her eyes made a more thorough survey of Romy, taking in Romy's deliberately understated suit and pearls. She smiled beautifully, pityingly. 'But you are certainly growing up, my dear.'

'Yes,' Romy agreed flatly, 'I certainly am.'

They sat in a civilised group on the expansive sofas by the window, while a servant brought champagne and a huge silver tray of Sicilian almond pastries.

'But you haven't *redecorated* the place,' Eva accused brightly, sipping champagne and looking around her. 'It's all just the same as the day I walked out of here. I was expecting the new broom to have swept clean!'

'Why?' Romy asked.

Eva's eyes met hers mockingly. 'Well, I'm sure it must give you the creeps, darling. You're far too young and pretty to be caged in this gloom.'

'I don't find the house at all gloomy,' Romy said, trying not to take the bait. 'I'm very happy here. Young as I am.'

The lie was of such monumental proportions that she was able to let it out without blinking. She met Xavier's ironic glance without flinching.

'Of course you are happy,' Eva laughed. 'Xavier just *adores* you, I'm sure, and he is a man who knows very well how to make a woman happy. Don't you, darling?'

'I do my best.' Xavier smiled. 'Not everyone shares your obsession with sweeping away the past, Eva. Perhaps Romy has more affinity with art than you do.'

If he was aware of the feminine tension in the air, he gave no sign of it. But it did not escape Romy that her husband's eyes were consistently drawn to the glittering, willowy figure of Eva. Why not? With a spasm of bitterness, Romy knew that she was, as she'd feared, just fading drably into the background. Her choice of grey and pearls had been wrong. She should have gone for a cool, summery pastel, something that would have been harder for Eva's firefly yellow to eclipse . . .

'The Ferrari, darling.' Eva's long fingers were stroking her ex-husband's. 'It's going *so* badly. Can't you have a word with the agency about it? They keep telling me there's nothing wrong with it. They think,' she said, turning briefly to Romy, 'that because I'm a mere *woman*, I know nothing about machinery. But I keep telling them, I am not an Italian woman, I am a German woman, and I *know* about cars.' She turned back to Xavier. 'Won't you speak to them, Zavi?'

'If you like,' Xavier agreed. 'What's the problem?'

Romy sat unmoving as Eva detailed a long list of vague defects in the car, her hand always on Xavier's. Anger was rising in her like lava. The assured intimacy between these two was more painful than she could possibly have anticipated. It made her feel helpless, shut out in a dark, cold place. There was none of the acid bickering that characterised some divorced couples. Rather, these two were like a well-matched pair of lovers, with Romy as the intruder.

'Very well.' Xavier nodded. 'Leave the car here today. The chauffeur will drive you home tonight in the Daimler, and tomorrow I'll take the car into the agent.'

'You are always such a darling.' With a melting smile for her ex-husband, Eva turned back to Romy. 'You don't mind, of course?'

'No. Why should I?' Romy smiled emptily into the triumphant green eyes.

'Darling, not all second wives are as civilised as you,' Eva cooed. 'But we were talking about the house. Now, there must be no argument. You *must* redecorate the place.' Eva licked the sugar off her fingers, and took another almond pastry out of the silver dish. 'Heaven knows, it needs it. I shall help you with everything, of course. I should have done it myself, years ago. But I shall take *such* pleasure in helping you do it now!'

'I rather like the place, as a matter of fact.' Romy was trying not to clench her teeth as she spoke. 'And I've only been married a week. I think that's a little soon to start making sweeping changes. Even with your able assistance. Don't you?'

'That's just where you're *wrong*.' Eva pointed an almond biscuit at her. 'Don't be intimidated by all the years of dust and history. They told me that the wallpaper in my villa is eighteenth century, but I'm having it ripped off all the same.' She tilted her platinum head at Romy. 'I can't *bear* fusty old furnishings. I'm having the whole place done out a beautiful, clean yellow, and I'm sending *dozens* of gloomy old antiques to the dealers.'

'Really?'

'They came with the villa. Supposed to be rococo, but I think they're nineteenth-century reproductions.'

'They were rococo,' Xavier said firmly. 'What you're doing is vandalism on a large scale, Eva.'

'Sweetie, I come from a long line of vandals. You know that.' She wrinkled her nose at Xavier. 'Anyway, I'm having the most fabulous new suite of furniture made in Torino, all upholstered in gold brocade. Just what this place needs. Tell you what . . . I'm going to send their little man to speak to you, dear girl. He has such *marvellous* ideas——'

'Please don't,' Romy said thinly. 'He would be wasting his time. I have no intention of changing the house, and I wouldn't dream of starting without consulting Xavier.'

Xavier smiled non-committally, and put down his glass. 'I'm going to have to leave you two to chat,' he announced, rising. 'Unfortunately, I must meet some boring people from Paris for an hour or two. But I'm sure you will get on like old friends.'

'I'm sure we will,' Romy said.

Xavier, impervious to her irony, took his leave of them with his usual courtesy. Eva sighed dramatically as the door closed behind him.

'Oh, I miss him,' she informed Romy. Her eyes met Romy's. 'All other men are like pasteboard imitations after Xavier, you know that?'

Romy picked up the bottle, trying to resist the awful impulse to brain the other woman with it. 'Some more champagne?'

'Please. It's the only alcohol I ever drink, you know. On my doctor's orders.'

'He sounds like a good doctor to have.'

'Darling, I can't tell you how many I went through before I found him. He's marvellous, I assure you. He insists that I eat at least an ounce of caviare a day. Russian, not that Persian stuff. Apparently I need the protein.'

'I'm sure you do. But tell me how you're having your villa done,' Romy invited. 'It sounds very interesting indeed.'

Twenty minutes later, Eva was still in full flood. There was nothing she liked so much, Romy had by now realised, as talking about herself, her plans, her possessions and her life. The calm arrogance of the woman was intimidating. Eva von Schimmel was used to the very best out of life. She had the manner and the attitudes of a princess. And her tastes were to match: very definite and very expensive.

Romy, having assessed the Dior silk, the leopard-skin coat and a flashy diamond brooch that twinkled on Eva's lapel—not to mention the Ferrari—found herself wondering bitterly whether Xavier was still supporting this expensive life-style.

'I went back to Düsseldorf two years ago,' she was sighing, 'but I missed Sicily so much. I hate German winters. Sometimes I hate everything about Germany, now. With just a *little* more money, I could be so happy here.'

'Could you?' Romy asked politely.

'But of course you don't have to worry about such things, my dear.' Narrowed green eyes considered Romy over the champagne glass. 'You haven't even realised how rich you are yet. I enjoy my independence, but I *adored* going around in a limousine, with a uniformed chauffeur, and being called *Baronessa*!'

'Still, you don't seem to be doing too badly,' Romy said with a hint of dryness.

'A Ferrari is nice, but it isn't a Daimler. And a villa isn't a *palazzo*.' She sighed theatrically. 'But one can be happy, just listening to the birds and smelling the almond blossom. I love everything about this island—the air, the people, the food. I can't resist the sweets. *Canoli* and *pastareale* and *pignola* . . . I'm terribly lucky. I can eat platefuls of the stuff, and not put on an ounce.' Eva's figure was slight, with curves in all the right places, none the less. She gave Romy's bust a critical look. 'You, of course, will have to avoid such things. You have a pound or two to lose, or am I wrong?'

'I think you're wrong,' Romy said evenly. There was only a touch of colour on her cheekbones to show that Eva was getting through to her.

'So. Perhaps you're content the way you are.' Eva's expression showed that *she* would have been far from content with Romy's figure. She leaned forward interlacing her long fingers. 'And here you are. How did Zavi propose to you?'

The question wasn't one that could be answered easily, and Romy's mouth tightened. 'He has been a friend of my family's for a long time,' she said neutrally. 'You know that.'

'It was not an extended courtship.' The green eyes were as sharp and hard as broken glass. 'You'll forgive me, *darling*, but I had never considered you as a possible wife for Zavi until a few weeks ago. I thought of you—if I thought of you at all—as a girl. I hardly had time to get used to the idea that Zavi was getting married again before it had happened.'

'It was certainly quick.' Romy straightened the pleats of her skirt. 'Xavier is a man of quick decisions, as I'm sure you know.'

'Do you know what I think?'

Romy was wary. 'About what?'

'About you and Xavier. I think that such a quick marriage can have only two explanations. Either he is utterly

besotted with you, or he doesn't give a damn about you.'
Eva sat back, after having delivered that bombshell, and
smiled into Romy's face. 'Now, I wonder, which is it?'

It was a struggle to keep her temper. 'Perhaps the answer
lies somewhere between the two extremes.'

'It usually does,' Eva agreed. She took a cigarette from
her bag, and blew a plume of smoke upwards, giving Romy
the benefit of her beautifully slender throat.

Romy watched her with tight-strung nerves. In the past
half-hour she had been given ample time to make her mind
up about Eva von Schimmel. Whatever snide comments
Xavier had to make about Paul Mortimer, this woman was
every bit as shallow and trivial as Paul had been. More, Eva
had a wide vicious streak in her, and she was not ashamed to
show it.

But then, Eva was stunningly beautiful, and gifted with a
unique, catlike sensuality that would make up, in a man's
view, for many failings.

Above all, Romy knew in her heart that Eva von
Schimmel did not feel like a divorced woman. The way she
talked to Xavier, the way she behaved with him, all
indicated that she had not finished with him yet, and that she
regarded that place in the chauffeured Daimler as exclusively
her own.

The thought was like a hammer-blow to Romy's heart.
She had a quick, unexpectedly sharp pang of pain as she
thought of this willowy blonde in bed with Xavier. They
would have gone well together. Eva was uninhibited enough
to make an electrifying sexual partner, and she would have
had none of Romy's hang-ups or tensions.

She had ridiculed her own dark suspicions that this woman
and her husband were still powerfully attracted to one
another, but now that possibility seemed very real indeed.

Suddenly she felt cold all over, as though her body had been
encased in ice.

CHAPTER SIX

'COLD?' asked Xavier as a shudder made Romy hunch her back. Without waiting for an answer, he slid a strong arm around her shoulders, and drew her close to his side. It was the first spontaneous gesture of any warmth that he had made all day, and she felt almost shocked at the contact for a moment. She felt her heart stir, her breasts tingling in a sensual response.

They were in the pale pink salon, a fire burning warmly in the grate, flooding the room with its glow. From the dining-room, the sounds of the servants clearing away their evening meal from the long oak table came faintly. 'This house is cold in winter,' he said, his body warm against hers. 'Next year, perhaps, we will put in central heating.'

'That would be nice,' Romy said stiffly. Touching him like this was making her heart thud unevenly, and she didn't welcome the disturbance.

'The cold weather doesn't last long here, of course. In a few weeks the dry wind will start blowing from Africa, and sweep all the clouds away. The almond blossom will be like white and pink foam, and all the hills will be covered in asphodels.'

'You don't have to talk about the weather,' she interrupted in a strained voice.

'What?'

'I'm not some maiden aunt who needs entertaining. I'd rather you said nothing than made small talk to me.'

He glanced at her, but didn't comment. She pulled away from his enclosing arm, and turned to face him, her

117

eyes shining with sudden tears. 'You've been treating me like—like an *object* all day. You haven't said a word to me about anything except platitudes about the weather, or whether I want another cup of coffee . . .'

'And that's so terrible?' he asked drily.

'You know what I mean! You behaved to *her* as though she were still mistress here, and to me as though I hardly existed at all!'

'You're overwrought,' he said in a bored tone, his eyes watching her from under lowered lids.

'You deliberately set out to exclude me! You spent over an hour and half with her, closeted in your study, while I twiddled my thumbs in the salon. What the hell were you talking about all that time?'

'Eva and I had some private business,' he said smoothly. 'I told you.'

'Too private for your wife to hear? And don't smile at me with that affable mask in place, Xavier. I know how you despise me inside——' Romy broke off, feeling that she must be crazy to spill out her vulnerability, exposing herself to his contempt.

'So?' he asked gently. 'How do you want me to look at you and speak to you?'

'With sincerity,' she said retorted. 'I'd prefer your real feelings to any amount of bogus pleasantries!'

'What if my real feelings *are* pleasant ones?'

'They're not.'

'This is a most interesting fit of humility, Romy,' he said with impatience. 'Must you always be either a queen or a beggar?'

She leaned against the marble fireplace, her blue eyes vivid in her pale face. 'Just for once, don't lie to me, Xavier. If you set out to punish me for last night, then you've done it very effectively. But that's not the way I do things. I'd rather it was out in the open! Tell me I behaved like a tramp last night. Tell me you care more about Eva's little finger than about my whole being! Just don't keep up with this charade!'

'Why should I say all that?' he asked calmly.

'Because it's true!'

Romy was shaking. She gulped back the stupid tears that were threatening to brim over. 'I just hate knowing how you feel about me, and having you cover it with politeness and smiles. I'd rather be treated with contempt than with politeness!'

'I don't think you would,' he said coolly. He slid his hands into the pockets of his jacket, and faced her with that unspoken challenge, legs slightly spread. 'Your problem is not a surfeit of humility, but a surfeit of pride. "I'd rather be treated with contempt than with politeness",' he mimicked her cruelly. 'The truth is that you must always be clamouring for attention, like a child. You have to be the centre of interest, and if you aren't, you slump into a fit of pique.'

'That's not true!'

'I think it is. Your jealousy of Eva was embarrassingly obvious today.'

'Are you surprised?' Romy said, her voice rising. 'The way she treated me, as though I were a stupid new servant who needed instructing in everything——'

'She behaved impeccably,' Xavier cut in shortly.

'Impeccably?'

'It was *you* who did not. You sulked like a spoiled child, which is exactly what you are most of the time. The truth is that you're hungry for attention, and you don't care whether it takes the form of kicks or kisses.'

'I just want honesty!'

'Hasn't it occurred to you that I may be treating you exactly as I feel?' He cocked his dark head on one side, as though assessing the effect of his words. 'Hasn't it occurred to you that my feelings for you are neither contemptuous nor affectionate, but just indifferent?'

Romy dropped her head to hide the tears that were swimming in her eyes. She'd asked for that, but it had hurt bitterly. 'Is that what you really feel for me?' she asked. 'Indifference?'

'I don't feel contempt,' he said, unmoved by her obvious distress. 'On the other hand, I'm not an infantile boy like Paul Mortimer, blathering about love. So perhaps indifference is the best way of summing it up, yes.'

'And what do you feel about Eva?' Why was she doing this to herself? She cared nothing for him. Why the hell should she give a damn what he felt about her? But some self-destructive force was pushing the words out of her lips. She looked up blindly, her face almost pleading. 'Something more?'

'Ah.' His eyes narrowed to shadowy slits. 'And this is the core of everything. You want me to say I desire you more than my ex-wife?'

'*No*. I wasn't asking you for crude sexual compliments, Xavier. I was simply making a request that you treat me with a little common honesty. But I see I was wasting my time. Honesty isn't a part of your character.' She turned away, tasting bitterness in her mouth. Why had she been so stupid as to expose herself to insult and humiliation like that? This would be the last time, she vowed, that she would ever show her true feelings for him. 'I'm going upstairs,' she announced in a dry voice.

His fingers bit into her shoulder, spinning her round like a leaf in the wind, and she found herself staring up into Xavier's face.

'There is a vital point for you to grasp,' he said in a controlled voice. 'And it is this: you have to resolve your own feelings, Romy. I am doing all I can to show you that

I want to be a husband to you. I can do no more. You must search your own heart, and understand the truth about your own emotions. You say we have nothing in common, that I bought you like a slave; I think that we have more in common than you dare admit. I think your heart is closed with a padlock, and that you have lost the key.' He slapped the marble of the fireplace, and she flinched. 'But here we are, my dear, man and wife. Whether we hate or love one another, we have taken a step together that can not be taken back again.' He took her chin in his fingers, and lifted her tear-streaked face so that he could stare into her brimming eyes. 'Tantrums will not cancel our marriage. These things mean nothing to me. I intend this marriage to last a damned sight longer than my last one. You understand me?'

She glared at him tearfully for a second, then fumbled in her pockets for a handkerchief. He supplied his own for her, and she blotted her eyes in silence.

'You must work it out for yourself,' he said grimly. 'Otherwise, we are going to go on playing this game *ad nauseum*. I have the patience for it. I don't think that you do.'

'It isn't a game,' she said in a shaky voice.

'No. It is not. But perhaps you need reminding of that more than I do.'

He smiled at her without warmth, and left her.

Alone, Romy turned to the mirror that hung over the fire, and mechanically arranged her hair. The face that looked back at her was cold and pale. Like a woman made of marble. She met her own deep blue eyes, seeing the unhappiness and confusion that clouded them. She dried her tears with Xavier's handkerchief, then crumpled the square of fine linen in her fingers, and tossed it into the fire.

She sank into the sofa in front of the fire, and hugged

herself, staring with unseeing eyes into the yellow core of the flames.

It was not until the preparations for the big party on Saturday night that she was able to feel the cloud lifting from over her.

Xavier had warned her that it was a big occasion, but she hadn't really understood how big until Friday afternoon, when she saw the trestle-tables being laid out on the lawn, and the huge striped marquee being erected, its top on a level with the roof of the great house. This was something special.

The outfit she chose on Saturday night was a figure-hugging black evening dress from Paris that was flatteringly low-cut to reveal her fine arms and shoulders, and to do more than just hint at her superb bust. She knew that it was more suitable for a West End première than this pagan, open-air festival, but she was determined to make an impression tonight, of all nights.

Warning her that the air might be cool, Xavier presented her with an exquisite Sicilian silk shawl that had been hand-embroidered with gold thread. He made no overt comment on the way she looked, but if his smoky gaze was anything to go by he didn't exactly disapprove.

By nine o'clock, the party was in full swing.

The bonfire roared, sweeping a continual vast cloud of sparks into the night sky above. The heat was tangible from twenty yards away, and the glare had turned the garden into a flood of orange light, peopled with a throng of dancing, chattering couples.

Contending with the constant roar of the fire, the orchestra—fiddles, tambourines and a mandolin that flickered and sparkled like the sparks themselves—was providing an endless stream of folk melodies. Romy estimated that there must easily be three hundred people present, turning the night into a feast of noise, music and laughter.

On the other side of the garden a pit had been dug and filled with coals, and over it several sheep were being roasted. The delicious smell of crisp lamb, spiced with rosemary and thyme, drifted in the air.

The long table she was sitting at glittered with crystal and silver. Family and close friends had been put here, under the pergola, though right now almost all of them except the very elderly were whirling round the fire in a *tarantella* that looked very giddy indeed. The bonfire was shedding enough heat to permit bare female shoulders, and to make the men's faces shine, despite the crisp night air.

The guests who had been crowding around her had eased off towards the fire for a while. Xavier, who had been at her side until now, had also left to dance with another woman; and Romy had found herself in a brief oasis of peace and quiet, for which she was grateful rather than otherwise.

She watched her husband's figure, tall among the crowd, dark against the flames. Her eyes were thoughtful, almost soft. Looking back over the fortnight that had passed since that heart-wrenching wedding in London, she'd been aware of many new emotions in herself.

The atmosphere tonight seemed to encapsulate everything that was strange and new in this new land. It was like nothing she had ever known, charged with a primitive joy that was hard to resist.

And she herself was very much a part of the celebration. It had been strangely touching to find herself the centre of attention, to realise that everyone here tonight wanted her to be happy. Those she'd already met in the past couple of weeks were by now old friends, and tonight she'd met literally dozens more. It was useless trying to remember all the names. But by this stage most of the faces that passed in the firelight, flushed with dancing and wine, were familiar.

She'd danced with more men than she could remember! Tomorrow her feet were going to ache, but tonight it was intoxicating to be so much in demand . . .

Her moment of solitude didn't last long.

Romy got to her feet for the umpteenth time as yet another family arrived at her table to greet her. Xavier was not at her side to help with the introductions, but there was scarcely any need. What with everyone talking at once, and the flood of hand-kissing and compliments, there was no need for shyness. Sicilians had a natural capacity for being happy, and it didn't matter that she could sometimes hardly follow their dialect; it was obvious by their smiling faces what they were saying to her.

At last, Xavier arrived to help her out. In the black evening-suit, he looked utterly magnificent. His beauty was of a dramatic kind; it needed an occasion like this, fiery and a little wild, to set it off. Tonight he looked every inch the Sicilian baron: dark, unbelievably handsome, and not quite of the modern era. Realising that this man was her husband made her heart falter in her breast, skipping a beat with a shiver.

When they were alone together, he looked down at Romy with eyes which reflected the flickering flames of the bonfire, and held out his hand to her.

'Dance with me.'

She slipped off her embroidered shawl and, taking his hand, went with him towards the fire.

His arms were so strong, yet they swept her into the dance with the gentleness of some great bird's wings. It was a fast waltz, almost a quickstep, and as he whirled her round the fire she had the giddy feeling that her feet were hardly touching the ground. Slightly light-headed, she gasped aloud, clinging to his broad shoulder. Xavier smiled down at her.

'You're beautiful tonight,' he murmured in his husky voice. 'Beautiful, but cool, like a woman made of marble. I'm almost surprised to feel that your flesh is soft and warm under my fingers.' His fingertips trailed gently over the silky skin of her spine, spreading to caress the smooth swell of her dorsal muscles, feeling the ripple of their movements as she danced.

'I'm not very good at waltzes . . . sorry if I'm clumsy.'

'You're like thistledown.' His mouth managed to brush her temple in a caress that wasn't quite a kiss. 'You dance like an angel.'

Whether it was his closeness, or what he said, or the proximity of the huge fire, Romy felt her skin flushing warmly. She smiled up at him quickly, her cheeks filling with colour. 'So many compliments? The champagne must have gone to your head!'

'Perhaps. What were you thinking of while you sat there alone just now? Your face was pensive.'

'I was thinking about this party. About all these new people, and what they must think of me.'

'Don't be worried. You're being the gracious hostess to perfection. You are the most beautiful woman here, too, and that's as it should be. Stop thinking, and just enjoy yourself!'

She could feel the hard muscles of his stomach and thighs moving against her. The arms that held her were so powerful and caressing, and the warmth of his mood enveloped her like a flame.

Sensual weakness stole over her like a treacherous spell, filling her with a heady desire she knew all too well. For a week they had lived without a touch of physical contact, and this romantic closeness was like wine on an empty stomach.

'And you?' she asked. 'What have you been thinking about tonight?'

'About you.' He held her slightly closer, steering her away from the crowd. 'Do you not find it strange that we two have never danced together before tonight?'

'Strange? Yes, I suppose so. You didn't exactly regale me with a long and tender courtship, did you?'

'You can't blame me for that,' he countered with a smile. 'You were the one who insisted on dispensing with the wooing. For all you know, I may have had all sorts of elaborate and romantic preliminaries planned for you before I popped the question. Furs and jewels and trips to Vienna. Soft music and bright lights to turn that pretty head of yours.'

'Did you?' Her expression reflected her reaction of uncertainty. 'I don't know whether you're teasing me or not.'

'Well,' he said drily, 'I certainly didn't plan on proposing to you in quite the way I ended up doing. Let's say that I was banking on a period of mutual acquaintance. But things didn't turn out that way.'

'I wasn't the snow-white maiden of your imaginings, was I?' she asked wryly, picking up something in his eyes.

'Well, I was a little taken aback when your father told me you'd just been through a torrid affair with a married man,' Xavier said in a dry voice.

Her quick eyes didn't miss the way his face tightened as he spoke. 'This is the twentieth century,' she reminded him defensively. 'And I didn't know he was married until it was too late. Anyway, I don't see why you should be so high and mighty. Haven't you had dozens of affairs since the divorce?'

'It's different for a man,' he growled.

'That old chestnut!' she exclaimed. 'Why is it all right for a man to be as promiscuous as he pleases, yet shocking and awful when a woman has one affair?'

'You were not a woman,' he pointed out shortly. 'You were a teenager.'

'Nineteen,' she said. 'Hardly a child.'

'As for all my so-called "affairs", don't be misled by what the newspapers print about me. Ninety per cent of it is just fabrication.' He looked at her sharply. 'Besides which, it is not the same thing. I am divorced, and thirty-one years old. You were little more than a child!'

She dropped her eyes. Given his old-fashioned attitude towards women and marriage, her fling with Paul was probably something of a shock for him to accept. 'Were you very angry?'

'I could have put you over my knee and——' His eyes glittered. 'Yes, I was angry.'

'Why?' she challenged practically. 'It wasn't as though we were even engaged, or anything.'

'In my mind,' he said emphatically, 'it was as though you'd betrayed me. But I want to show you something. Let's get away from the crush.'

Xavier eased Romy away from the heat and noise of the bonfire. It was like coming down to earth after flying; her legs felt leaden and slow as he escorted her through the throng of smiling people. They let themselves in through one of the french doors, into a side drawing-room. It was empty. Another fire was burning here, a fire tamed and confined by the marble fireplace, but otherwise the room was dark. Xavier switched on a table-lamp, and in the soft light turned to her, with something in the palm of his hand.

'I never gave you an engagement ring. It hardly seemed appropriate at the time. But now . . .'

Numbly, she took the little velvet box, and prised it open. The firelight leaped suddenly into her hands, glittering in the facets of the diamond, glowing with an unearthly radiance.

She stared at the ring stupidly. It didn't require much expertise to tell that the diamond was very big and of superb quality. It seemed to shed, rather than refract, the light. She was motionless for so long that he took the ring from her, and slid it over her wedding finger.

'Do you approve?' he asked, kissing her cold lips.

'Xavier——' Suddenly, her eyes were filled with tears. The gift had touched her more than she knew how to express. She didn't deserve anything as precious as this.

She reached up to pull his neck down, her mouth seeking his. It was the first kiss she had willingly given him, and it was almost clumsy in its intensity. She spread her slender fingers slowly through his hair, feeling the crisp, springy resistance under her palm. His physical beauty was intoxicating, but there was more to it than that; what was growing between them was a true desire, a desire born out of mutual need and mutual understanding.

As he drew back to look down at her, she felt that she had never been closer to any man.

'I would give you diamonds every day,' he said softly, 'if I thought they would earn me a kiss like that.'

She reached up and traced the curve of his lips with her fingertips, as though marvelling at what his kiss could do to her. 'You're a very special man.'

Xavier drew his finger down the arch of her throat, to the scented hollow of her collarbone. 'You're so beautiful,' he said softly. 'You know how you make me feel, don't you?'

She could only stare up at him, as though mesmerised.

'But I will possess my soul in patience until we are alone.' His face was smiling, his eyes smoky with what he felt for her. 'We can't hide in here all night. People will talk. We must go back to our guests.'

'I'm ready,' she told him, looking up at him.

He took her arm, and escorted her back into the night air.

It was cool on her flushed skin, but didn't help to bring her back to her senses. Normality was a long way away as they walked back to the table.

Long past midnight, when the last dance had been danced, and all the guests had wended their way homeward, she and Xavier lay in bed, staring into one another's eyes.

'Romy, you've made me proud of you tonight . . .'

She felt his lips touch her neck, his hands drawing the cloud of black hair away from her face.

She could smell the faint tang of burning oakwood from the fire. It was as if nothing else existed but the two of them, in this firelit room . . .

His body was hard with desire, and his mouth sought hers with ardent male hunger. And tonight, for the first time, her own response was unhesitating. Giving a little moan, she pressed to him with a desire that was almost frantic in its intensity, clinging to him as though for comfort.

He took her with an overwhelming gentleness, his kiss melting her like ice in the sun. It was so good to be with him, so good to cling to his male strength, to mould her slender body against him, and feel his weight press on her breasts.

Their lovemaking unfolded in a sea of fire, obliterating all thought, all doubt. There was no power to resist in her now. In the past week he had turned her from a cold and uncooperative maiden into an eager voluptuary, who craved the very thing she had set her mind to despise.

As their bodies closed in the *paso doble* of love, Romy felt her soul lifted by a sensation of beauty, of perfection. She pressed against Xavier as though wanting to drown herself in him, her heart and body driven by a gnawing fear that this moment must never be lost again. He made her feel so much, so very much . . . if this was not a true marriage of souls, then what was it? Could any mere physical passion move her as strongly as this, or stir her inmost heart so fiercely?

It was a long time before it was over. Finally, she lay in his arms with thudding heart and quickened breath, the spinning world settling slowly back to normality around her. Xavier did things to her that she had never dreamed could be possible. In all her experience with Paul, she had never even approached the heights that she soared above now.

How insane that she'd ever thought she would be able to stay indifferent to Xavier.

When she'd embarked on this strange marriage, she had imagined a life in which he would play only a minor role. All her thoughts had been about herself, about herself and her petty wishes. She'd never thought of this agreement as a marriage. It had been an arrangement, something cold-blooded and clearly defined, that contained no emotion. She would go her way and he would go his, and nothing inside her would ever really change.

Had she really imagined she could lead her own existence here in Sicily, following her own path without reference to Xavier?

She had underestimated him by a factor of about a million. Even before Paul, Xavier de Luca had had an impact on her that was unlike anything she'd known before. What he'd thought and said had mattered to her, had mattered with an intensity that made all her resolutions turn into nonsense. His disapproval, his approval, his criticism or his praise, these were things that could plunge her into despair or fill her with delight.

He affected her. His influence was potent and subtle, and at times he made her feel like a marionette, her captive emotions lifting or sinking obediently at his effortless command.

Right from the start, Xavier had fascinated her. As a child, as a girl, as a developing adolescent, he had loomed large and dark in her thoughts, a person of profound significance in her life.

And, from that morning in the Athenaeum, she had known in her heart that their destinies were forever bound together.

Looking back now, she was starting to see just how shallow and insubstantial her relationship with Paul had been. She'd imagined herself so badly hurt. She'd even convinced herself that she could never love again. Such schoolgirlish melodrama! She hadn't had the faintest idea what a real man was like, or how powerful a mature sexual relationship could be. If what she'd had with Paul had been anything like this, then yes, she would have been savagely hurt by his betrayal. But it hadn't been.

Being close to Xavier was putting a lot of things in proportion. With hindsight, she could see how much her feelings for Paul had been self-delusion, romantic fantasies. She'd been in love with the idea of love, not with a man of flesh and blood. Next to Xavier, Paul had been as insubstantial as a cinema image, a thing made out of imagination and illusions. And her love for him, likewise, had been more in theory than in practice.

How much of her bitter grief over Paul, she now wondered, had been just self-dramatisation? How much had been play-acting, or at best, piqued pride? One couldn't compare her relationship with Paul to Xavier's relationship with Eva. She had been through a hollow affair. They had had a marriage which had, if nothing else, lasted two years.

Did it really matter how they'd come together? After all, arranged marriages had been the norm for hundreds of years, and sometimes they could work out for the best . . .

'What are you thinking?' he asked, kissing her brooding forehead.

'About us,' she answered dreamily.

'Good,' he murmured, drawing her close. 'You've got a lot of thinking to do. But sleep now, my love. It's been a long day.'

CHAPTER SEVEN

OVER the next fortnight, Romy was aware that their relationship had changed radically.

Or, to put it more accurately, it had developed from point zero to something that much more significant.

In bed, it went without saying, they were fantastic together. As they learned about one another's bodies, their lovemaking acquired a luminosity, an intensity that was starting to shed a glow through her whole being. She even looked different, to the extent that Xavier had commented on her radiant eyes and flawless complexion.

As the days passed, she was able to see further into her husband's character than ever before.

Since the night of the bonfire, she'd started feeling very differently towards him; and the incredible thing was that he seemed to care about her. If what he'd said had contained any truth at all, his feelings for her went deeper than anything she'd envisaged, or even wanted. With girlish petulance, she'd refused to believe that he could ever become close to her. The age gap between them, alone, had seemed an insuperable barrier.

But now . . . now she felt that she might have misjudged him. Maybe none of those obstacles really mattered, after all.

For one thing, he understood her more than she knew. She'd thought herself so opaque, so difficult to know; yet as time passed Romy began to see just how well Xavier really knew her. It was as though he had some instinctive ability to read her inmost emotions, emotions that went too deep for thought or word to explain. Up until now,

she had disliked him. She had feared his strength, his
authority, his capacity to hurt her. She had hated him for
reasons which hadn't been real at all.

He was an extraordinary man, with a man's strength
and pride, and it would take her time to get close to him,
just as it was taking him time to get close to her. The real
obstacle to closeness, though, lay not in him, but in her.
She had to learn to trust him, and she had to gain enough
confidence in herself to feel that she could make him a
generous and caring wife. That was where the rub lay,
because self-confidence and trust were two qualities she
was particularly short on.

And, most difficult of all, she had to learn to try and
cancel out their bad beginning, try to start again. With
regard to that, she didn't have the faintest idea where to
start.

Perhaps the crucial truth lay in understanding that she
herself could mean something in his life—that there was a
place for her, an important one, and that he was simply
waiting for her to step into it. But could she really do so?

Being his wife was one thing.

Being a mother to his children was quite another.

She was under no illusions that, if things went on as
they did, she would soon be pregnant. And that was a
prospect that frightened her.

Bearing children was not in itself the thought that
disturbed her. It was that she knew she still lacked the
depth of commitment, the feeling of trust in Xavier. She
was drawn to him, moved by him deeply; but in her
inmost soul she could still not bring herself to trust him
that far. She didn't know him that well; and, to be utterly
frank, she didn't know herself that well, either. To bear
his children was a step that needed more confidence and
less confusion than she presently faced. A *lot* less.

Once there was a child involved, she would be tied to

Xavier far more tightly, and with far less chance of escape. She could not forget his grim warning, all those weeks ago, in London. 'The Italian courts will ensure that you are left with nothing. Not even your children. You may find that you are never allowed to be alone with them again. You accept this condition?

She didn't want a pregnancy yet. Being blunt, she would have preferred to take precautions until she had her feelings sorted out. But she dared not broach the subject to Xavier, not yet, at any rate. It would, besides being a flagrant violation of their deal, hurt and anger him deeply. And she was not the sort of woman who was able to do so privately, without telling him.

What could she do? It was a subject that preyed on her mind, and began to assume hauntingly large proportions.

Romy awoke drowsily one morning to find that their room was filled with sunshine.

Xavier was already awake, and as she looked up sleepily at him he tickled her nose with a lock of her own hair. Romy stretched languidly, a half-smile playing on her mouth.

'You look delicious,' he said huskily. 'I've been wanting to wake you, but you were such a pretty sight.'

'You can't be very fussy,' she murmured.

'Oh, I'm very fussy,' he assured her. 'And you suit me just fine.' He kissed her, a long and unmistakably desirous kiss. 'I've got the morning free,' he whispered.

'Have you?' she asked, smiling wider. 'What are you suggesting we do with it?'

'You mean afterwards?' he enquired, raising one eyebrow.

Romy giggled. 'Yes.'

'I thought we might go for a ride.'

'How lovely!' she exclaimed. 'It's been weeks since I

was on a horse—and I miss Dodo so much.'

With a rough murmur, he drew her close, his hands hungrily moulding her delicate, almost fragile body against his own.

She felt her mouth opening under his like a flower, admitting his tongue. It was warm in the bedroom—warm, secluded and intimate. Her body felt clean and smooth in his arms, and there was a kind of perfection about the moment.

Whispering her name, Xavier covered her face with kisses, his lips trailing down the line of her throat to the porcelain-fine span of her collarbone.

'My love,' he whispered, kissing her there, 'you're as beautiful as porcelain. Sometimes I'm afraid you'll break in my arms.'

'I'm not that fragile,' she whispered back. Her eyes were closed in ecstasy as he kissed her throat, her bare shoulders. 'I won't break . . . if you're careful with me . . .'

His mouth was seeking hers again, his arousal making his kisses more challenging, more demanding. Her lips, soft and moist now, opened and clung to his without opposition, allowing the secret inner caress of his tongue. She let him kiss her, rather than returning his kisses, lost in the bliss of being desired with such intensity.

To awake every morning like this . . . to be loved like this for the rest of her life . . . she couldn't have wished for greater ecstasy. Her movements were slow, luxurious, but her passivity hardly seemed to matter. He was totally in command, his lovemaking sure and urgent.

'Do you have any idea how much I want you?' he asked, smiling against her mouth.

'Xavier . . .' Her arms were around his neck, her fingers roaming slowly through his crisp, dark hair. There was a growing hunger in them both which spiked the gentleness of their caresses with craving.

In the silent intensity of this moment, it was as though they'd been together all their lives, as though nothing could ever part them.

Her own tongue moved against his. With growing urgency, her hands roamed across his back, hungry for the feel of his skin. It was hot and velvety under her palms, the muscles thrillingly hard and strong. She felt his hand caress her breast, tracing the taut curve under the silk. Desire leaped along her veins, like fuel exploding into flame. The want was there in her, the need to let him slake her hunger, to peel off her gown, and offer him her naked breasts, give him her jutting nipples, whisper to him to take them in his mouth . . .

She arched to Xavier, shutting her eyes as she felt him do what she had silently commanded. His mouth brushed the creamy curves of soft flesh, approaching the erect peaks with maddening slowness. She cradled his head in her arms, whimpering in tender complaint as she felt the harshness of his lips and teeth claiming her nipples, shuddering as the melting sweetness of his tongue made amends in a voluptuous, moist caress that brought even more torment.

His hand was warm on her belly. The combination of caresses, his mouth on her nipples, his hand there on her womb, moved Romy in a deep, irresistible way. When she half opened her eyes, they were swimming with wetness, and her voice was husky as she whispered his name again.

His palm slid downward over the silky plane of her loins, reaching the dark triangle of her sex, and cupped her with possessive fingers.

Romy felt a swelling ecstasy unfold as his fingers stirred, touching the melting flesh of her womanhood, expertly bringing an intensity of pleasure that made her cry out aloud. Her substance felt swollen under his touch, aroused beyond any limit she had known before.

Suddenly understanding that he was deliberately waiting for her to acknowledge what he was doing to her, she dug her fingernails into his hard shoulders, and whispered shakily, 'Yes! I want you . . . now . . .'

'Yes,' he said jaggedly, his breathing uneven. 'We have found one another, my love.'

His words struck a deep chord of truth within her. That she could ever have been repelled by him was incredible to her now. He was beautiful, the most magnificent man she had ever seen. She felt that her whole life had been a leading up to this marriage, to this encounter with this strange, potent man. From this time, her future led outward, to a new horizon, and regions she had never seen.

They made love with slow, exquisite warmth, reaching a conclusion that was shudderingly deep, yet filled with a strange serenity.

'My darling,' he said quietly, a long time afterwards, 'you do not know how I long to have a family with you.'

Romy flinched at the words. Sensing her reaction, he drew her close.

'Why did you pull that face? Has something I said upset you?'

'Of course not.' She tried to sound light, but he wasn't fooled. 'I was just . . .'

'Just what?'

'I was just a little disturbed when you said that. About a family.'

'Don't you want children?' he asked quietly.

'It's not that easy to explain my feelings. I don't think you'd understand.'

He touched her lips with his fingertips. 'I understand that you're insecure and confused. But you were made for motherhood, Romy. It's what I want, almost more than anything else in the world . . .'

'Is that all I am to you?' she said in a voice that was slightly unsteady. 'A breeding machine? Something to be made pregnant as soon as possible?'

'Romy!' he said, brows descending at her tone and her expression. 'What the hell has got into you?'

'I thought you wanted *me*.' She sat up and pulled the tumbled cloud of her hair away from her face. The sweetness of desire at her loins was now an ache. But, now that the subject was here, she must face telling him the truth.

'I do want you,' he said with sharp emphasis. 'I want you as much as any man ever wanted a woman!'

'But you can't stop thinking about your heirs,' she retorted. 'You've just said it—that's what's most important to you!'

'Don't be absurd,' he growled. 'I don't understand how you can talk like this, after what we've just done together.'

'I'm just not in any tearing hurry for motherhood.' She turned to look at him over her naked shoulder, and her eyes were dark. 'Oh, yes, I know I swore I'd give you two children in London. That was the deal. But I want a little time. I'm not ready, Xavier. When I feel a little surer of myself . . . of us . . .'

His brows came down grimly. 'You mean you refuse to commit yourself to me that far.'

'I can't help the way I feel,' she protested, hugging herself tightly as she faced him. 'All I'm asking is for a little time. To fall pregnant to a man who is almost a stranger to you . . . it's a little frightening, a little disturbing. Please try and understand, Xavier,' she pleaded.

'Are you asking what I think you're asking?' he

demanded, eyes glittering.

'Well——' She was flushing scarlet. 'I don't want to stop making love, you know that. Perhaps it would be better if we took . . . precautions.'

The silence seemed to hiss, like a record that had come to an end. He got out of bed and walked to the shower in silence, his face as hard as a bronze mask.

She bit her lip, cursing herself for her clumsiness. Xavier was a sophisticated man, but he was also a Sicilian to his core, and her attitude would have been deeply, perhaps unforgivably, offensive to him. But she could not take the words back. She'd meant them. For pity's sake, how could he be so incredibly sensitive and loving in one moment, and so unfeeling in the next?

They showered and dressed in silence. As she brushed her hair, staring absently into space, Xavier came to sit beside her on the bed. She was expecting anger, but his face was serious.

'Tell me something. Do you believe in taking chances?'

She glanced at him curiously. 'I've taken chances all my life.'

'I have not,' he replied. 'I am a man who prefers certainties to gambles.' For a moment, his face was knotted in an intense frown. Then he gave a slight shrug, as though dismissing his doubts. 'But I'm going to take a chance with you now, Romy. I want to tell you something you should know.'

'What about?' she asked.

'About the circumstances around our marriage. Especially the financial circumstances. You've had a lot of things wrong, right from the start.'

'I don't understand.' She was sitting up, hugging the sheet round her knees. 'Wrong about what? You asked Papa for a share in the company——'

'I asked for nothing,' he cut in brusquely. 'You have to

understand that from now on.'

'But the money?' she queried.

'I offered to refloat the company as a matter of course. How could I offer to marry you, and leave your family to become paupers?' He shook his head. 'The idea would be inconceivable. I proposed an interest-free five-year loan of half a million pounds. I never asked for a slice of the company, Romy. It was your father who suggested that detail.'

'Papa?' she gasped.

'Of course.' He studied her from under brooding lids. 'You didn't really think I wanted to be *paid*, as you once so neatly put it, for marrying you? The idea was your father's. I tried to refuse, but he was extremely insistent. He seemed to feel that he couldn't take the money, that he had to give me something in return, though I assured him that wasn't the case at all. As you yourself said, he is a very old-fashioned man, with old-fashioned ideas of propriety.'

She was watching him with huge eyes, her heart pounding. 'What are you leading up to?'

'I eventually agreed that I would take certain rights in Forlari Wines, but I did it for the sake of your father's pride, and to help cement the two families together. I certainly had no intention of drawing money out of the company, either; I envisaged the share as being yours, a marriage portion which would belong to you, rather than me, and which would in time give you a considerable degree of financial independence.'

Her mouth had been hanging open in disbelief. 'Is that the truth?' she demanded dazedly.

'You can always check with your father,' he invited her calmly. 'When you, for your own part, insisted that I renounce any claims to the company, it made very little difference. Your father was simply forced to agree to the original arrangement I had proposed. I explained that you refused to accept that particular clause, and that there was no chance of working things out without your consent. So your father will pay me back the money when Forlari Wines is back in the black. Not that it had ever mattered to me. The real question at stake was, and had always been, yourself.'

Her skin felt hot and cold by turns. She lifted her hand to her forehead, trying to stop the pounding there.

'Are you all right?' Xavier asked in concern.

'I don't know,' she confessed dazedly. 'I'm lost for words.'

'That makes a change,' he said drily.

Romy tried to pull herself together, feeling as though the bottom had just dropped out of her world. 'Why—why haven't you ever told me this before?'

His smile was oblique, wry. 'I'd hoped it wouldn't be necessary. Your father and I made a mutual agreement to say nothing of this to you.'

'Why?'

'We had differing reasons,' Xavier replied. 'But they came to the same thing in the end, which was making you my wife.'

'What do you mean?'

'When we met that morning in the Athenaeum, it was immediately obvious to me that I wasn't going to get anywhere with you using the conventional language of proposal. You were extraordinarily antagonistic. Almost savage, in fact. Your family had warned me that you were very bitter about what Paul Mortimer had done to you, but they hadn't told me just how hostile you were towards me. At first I thought you had come there to refuse me.'

Romy watched his face in a taut silence as he paused to gather his thoughts.

'The most important thing to me,' he went on, 'was

that you obviously felt under considerable pressure about the whole thing.' He shrugged. 'Pressure of your own imagining, of course. But I knew that if that pressure were to be taken away, I had no hope at all of making you my wife. The pressure was my only ally in a losing situation.'

'So you lied to me!' she gasped.

'You lied to yourself,' he corrected her, with his old severity of manner. 'I simply stood by while you invented a complicated string of reasons for marrying me.'

'I don't believe this,' she said in an unsteady voice. She was reeling, dizzy. 'It was only ever a loan? And you've let me think I'd been bought, all this time?' She was dizzy to the point of swaying on her feet. 'You mean—you mean—*I needn't have married you at all?*'

'That's an entirely different matter,' Xavier said with a shadowy smile. 'The necessity of your marrying me was never in any doubt at all. Not to me, at any rate.'

'But—but I only agreed to marry you to save my father!' she cried.

'I cannot believe that,' he contradicted her gently. 'You love your father, yes. But such things cannot be done. A marriage means more than any number of millions. Nor could any compulsion be more important than the prompting of your own heart. You married me because you wanted to.'

'You're mad if you think that!' The irises of her eyes were so dark as to be almost indigo. The turmoil inside her was too big to be contained. The confused emotions of disbelief and betrayal were starting to spill out of her, uncontrolled. 'How could Papa have done this to me?'

'Your father loves you very deeply,' Xavier answered. 'He was facing bankruptcy and ruin, and his only thought was to provide you with a secure future before the crash came.'

'And you were only too keen to help out, weren't you?' she flared at him. 'It came naturally to you to lie!'

'Because I wanted you,' he retorted, his face urgent. 'Because otherwise, I would have lost you for ever.'

'And didn't I have any say in the matter? Was I just another chattel in one of your *deals*?' She was gasping for breath, as though the room was suddenly too close, suffocating her.

Impatience hardened his face. 'No, Romy. I'm trying to tell you exactly the opposite. You are the only one who talks about deals. You've got the idea fixed deep in your concept of our marriage. And I think this state of mind is very harmful. That is why you cannot trust me, and why you do not want children with me.'

'Is that why you told me this?'

'We have a real, living marriage, Romy,' he said urgently. 'Not a deal or an agreement. A marriage, with so much potential for love. Starting a family isn't a part of some contract—it's the natural consequence of being husband and wife. For pity's sake, stop thinking in terms of agreements or arrangements. Stop seeing me as some kind of heartless manipulator——'

'You're the arch-manipulator,' she spat at him. Her anger was blazing, but there were no more tears. Only purpose. Only a fierce determination. 'It's over, Xavier. This changes everything between you and me.'

'You are wrong.' His mouth was hard. 'Nothing has changed.'

'Our marriage means nothing now!'

'It has exactly the same meaning it had before you knew any of this,' Xavier said grimly. 'No more, no less.'

Her laugh sounded like a sob. 'I'm sure you can square what you've done with your conscience. But I can't. You *lied* to me. I'll never forgive you, never!'

He was watching her with smoky eyes. 'I see I should

have kept the truth to myself,' he said quietly.

'Yes!' she agreed. 'You should. I'm going back to England, Xavier. A divorce shouldn't be too hard to arrange. Our *marriage*——' she gave the word a biting emphasis '—has been based on a lie from start to finish.'

'You're wrong,' he contradicted quietly.

'*No*. I'm going back, Xavier.'

'Where to?'

'To London, of course. To my family.'

Xavier's mouth tightened in a smile that was gently mocking. 'Poor Romy. You cherish some odd illusions. Who will take you? Your father? Your brother? Do you really imagine your father would take you in, knowing you had deserted me, knowing that your place was here? As for your brother, Teo, he struck me as a man of little tolerance. I cannot see much hope in that direction. Your family would feel nothing but shame and dishonour if you were to go back now.'

'*Bastard!*'

He was as cool as ice. 'I'm sorry that you're taking it like this. I had the odd idea it might make you feel differently about me, and the idea of having children. But nothing has changed. Not for you, not for me, not for your family in England. They will never take you back if you leave me. They will tell you what I tell you now—that your place is with your husband. With me. That ceremony we went through is not so easily broken.' His voice grew harsher. 'It meant more than a few words or a signature on a page. You are my wife. And nothing has happened to change that.'

She'd listened in a taut silence. 'Of course something's happened to change it,' she said fiercely. 'We had an agreement——'

'The agreement was all in your own head,' he said ruthlessly. 'You agreed to marry me, and now we have a marriage.'

'The travesty of a marriage,' she snapped. 'I'm going to get a divorce!'

'On what grounds? Non-consummation? That works best if virginity can be proved, I'm afraid. Not so easy in this case. Abandoning me will only make things all the more difficult for you. And rest assured that if you go back to London, I will never co-operate in any divorce proceedings you may start. You will still be sitting in a lawyer's office in five years' time from now. You will find no freedom, only exposure and disgrace. And I can also assure you that neither your brother nor your father will take you in. They will turn you away from their door. You will be utterly alone.'

She gasped at the cold words. 'Damn you! You don't know my father, or you would never dare say such a thing about him!'

'*You* don't know your father,' Xavier contradicted her, unmoved, 'or you would not be talking like a fool. Your father is a Sicilian, a man of honour. You nearly broke his heart when you had that affair with Paul Mortimer.'

She laughed bitterly. 'Is that why he conspired with you to sell me, like a slave at market?'

'If there was any conspiracy, it was made out of love for you, Romy.'

'If he loves me, Papa could never turn me away. *Never*.'

Xavier's eyes narrowed. 'And what about the small matter of my five hundred thousand pounds? It is within my power to demand the return of that money at any time, Romy. That would mean the end of Forlari Wines, once and forever. Complete, utter destruction.

'You wouldn't!' she whispered, white-faced at the blow.

He made a gesture of contempt. 'If the thought of

being held a hostage here is such a turn-on for you, then there's no problem turning it into a reality.'

She shook her head numbly. After the warmth and closeness that had passed between them, it cut her to the soul that he could talk like this.

'If I were you, my love, I would think very hard before you book any tickets to London.' His eyes took in the rigid muscles of her throat and shoulders, and his expression gentled. 'I don't want to talk to you like this, Romy. I want you here, with me. And I cannot allow you to think that what you now know in any way cancels our marriage.' He touched her cheek with gentle fingers. 'It doesn't.'

'Don't *touch* me!' With the wildness of a trapped animal, she knocked his hand away. 'Don't come near me,' she hissed, glaring at his austere, tense face. 'I hate you! I'll always hate you!'

Romy and Xavier stared at one another in a bleak silence, neither able to look away. The tension seemed to sing like high-voltage cables in the wind.

It was Xavier who spoke first. 'I want to be your husband,' he said in a rasping voice. 'But you force me to be your enemy.'

'Does that surprise you?' she snarled at him. 'After the way you've treated me?'

'And what,' he said in a quietly savage voice, 'if I object to the way you treat *me*? What if I grow weary of your coldness, your insolence, your presumption? What if I grow impatient of waiting for you to have the *inclination* to start behaving like a wife.'

'Then throw me out of the house,' she shot back, 'like a good Sicilian husband! Send me back to England with your curse, and take up with Eva again! She'd like nothing better!'

'No.' White teeth glinted in a tiger's smile. 'Here you

are, and here you stay.'

'You'll regret it,' she panted, feeling the closest thing to hate she'd ever known. 'I'll make your life a misery!'

'Because you think you'll force me into letting you go?' His eyes were glinting ominously under his lowered brows. 'Wrong. I'm not such a fool.'

'I'll never let you make love to me again,' she raged at him. 'You broke your part of the bargain right from the start. Well, I'm breaking my part now! You can forget any thought of a family, because I'm never having a child of yours, not ever! I want my own bedroom. Do you hear me?'

'I hear you.' The emotion was gone from his eyes and mouth, and in its place was a steely firmness. His eyes were hard. 'I am detached from you, Romy. You have taken this too far. I feel nothing but indifference.' The words cut like a lash. 'I will instruct the servants to move my things to another bedroom today. That should make you happy, at least.'

She flung herself away from him, and buried her face in the pillows while he dressed in a tight silence.

As soon as he had left the room, she snatched up the telephone and punched in the number for England.

The voice that answered her call belonged to Laura, her sister-in-law. 'Papa and Teo are both at a meeting with the receiver, in the City,' she told Romy. 'They've been working day and night to get the firm on its feet again, and it's just starting to pay off. What's wrong, Romy? You sound upset. Has anything happened?'

Unable to keep in her hurt and sense of betrayal, Romy launched into a near-incoherent account of what she had just learned from Xavier.

After five minutes, Laura's voice cut in.

'Romy. *Romy!*'

Romy had been speaking with passion, and she paused

breathlessly, drained by the effort of spilling her feelings down the telephone. 'What?'

'I know all this.'

'Then you were in on it, too!' She wiped her wet eyelids clumsily. 'How could you all have done this to me?'

'You're upset,' Laura soothed gently. 'All you need is time to get used to the idea, and you'll realise how happy you could be.'

'Happy? *Here?* Never. Oh, Laura, do you think I wouldn't come home on the next flight if I could?'

'Don't ever do that. Papa would be dishonoured and ashamed,' Laura said, unconsciously repeating Xavier's words. 'If you only knew how much he hopes this marriage will work out . . .'

'Work out? How can it ever work out?' Romy demanded. 'There isn't anything *to* work out. There's no love in this house.'

'Then you'll have to make it,' Laura retorted. 'You don't know what you're talking about throwing away.'

'Oh, I think I do,' she answered acidly. 'I've thrown myself away already. What's left that has any meaning?'

'What nonsense. You've got your whole life to enjoy.'

Romy stared at the key-pad on the phone. As the rage drained out of her, she was feeling empty and beaten. 'My whole life? Not now. Not any more.'

'Xavier is a *wonderful* man,' Laura said urgently. 'But if you don't learn how to approach him, you may lose him for ever.'

'No such luck.' Romy lay back against the pillows. 'He'll never let me go. He said so this afternoon.'

'And do you think he's keeping you there for his own amusement?' Now it was Laura's turn to be ironic. 'He's a sophisticated, adult male with an extraordinary mind, and you're talking like an addle-brained adolescent!'

'And you're talking like a sentimental fool,' Romy snapped back, her grief flaring into anger. 'So he's charmed you, too, has he? This is no picture-book romance, Laura, with a happy ending on the last page. It's a travesty, a fraud. It's a trap which I know I'll never get out of. It doesn't have a chance.'

'Yes, it does,' Laura said with unexpected brusqueness. 'It *does* have a chance, Romy. I know about unsuccessful marriages. I have rather more experience than you do.'

Romy felt a pang of shame. 'I didn't mean——'

'It can't have escaped your notice,' her sister-in-law went on shortly, 'that Teo and I are not exactly a blissful combination. We married for reasons that seemed good enough at the time. Family reasons, business reasons. Well——' she shrugged briefly '—the reasons are still good, but the marriage isn't up to much. Maybe if I'd been able to have children, things would have turned out differently. But so far I haven't.'

'I didn't know,' Romy said quietly.

'If we'd had a child years ago, it might have drawn us together. But now it's probably too late. I wouldn't want to bring a child into a marriage without love, even if I could have one, which I probably can't. So there's another advantage you have over me. You can have children. I probably never will.'

'Oh, Laura,' Romy said gently, sitting up. 'I'm so sorry.'

'I'm not telling you all this to make you feel sorry for me,' Laura said, her voice gentling. 'Just believe that I know what I'm talking about. You say Xavier despises you. He doesn't. He cares about you. If you can't see that, you must be blind. He wanted to marry you years ago, and you've obviously been in his thoughts a long time. Whatever has gone wrong between you, and I don't want to pry into that, Xavier is man enough to give you the time and space to sort yourself out. Don't be a fool, Romy. Don't throw this marvellous chance away. If you let him, Xavier will give you the kind of marriage that women like me can only imagine. Do you know how many women dream about him? Can you imagine how many women would swap places with you tomorrow? He's the sexiest, cleverest, most beautiful man you'll ever meet. But he's proud. He has every right to be. And if you turn his respect for you to contempt, you'll have lost him for ever . . .'

'Oh, Laura,' Romy said tiredly, 'you don't understand. You never will . . .'

'I'm not going to tell your father about this call,' Laura said firmly. 'Give yourself a few days to settle down. Just after a monumental row is not the best time to think straight. If you need to talk, I'm always here. OK?'

Romy didn't answer for a moment. Then she sighed in sad resignation. 'Thanks for listening, anyway. I know you mean well.'

She hung up and sat where she was, staring into nowhere.

There was nothing she could say. She had been duped, tricked, deceived into a marriage by her family and by Xavier. What hurt most was the thought that Papa had connived at it all.

It wasn't hard to understand why he'd done it, of course. To his old-fashioned Sicilian way of looking at things, the scandal of her affair with Paul had been a profound shock. He'd obviously felt it an urgent duty to get her a respectable husband as soon as possible. Xavier was the dazzling choice.

And that sordid business about the money had been no more than an incidental issue, a red herring to obscure the real aim, which had been to marry her off to Xavier. She felt blinded, as though a window had just been opened into her heart, illuminating things that had been hidden for weeks.

The offer of a share in the firm had come from her father. Of course. Where else? Xavier, whatever else he might be, was not the kind of man who would ever have used money as a lever to blackmail Papa. He was no more capable of that than of cheating or theft.

She had rushed into this marriage so precipitately, so sure that she was the shining saviour of the hour.

What a sentimental fool she had been! What the hell had she thought it was? Some kind of good deed? A grandiose gesture, something she could unslip once it had begun to chafe her skin?

A knot of grief was in her throat. Self-pity welled up in her, flooding her eyes. She wouldn't be calling home again.

She'd hooked herself on to this barbed-wire cross—oh, yes, she had done it all unaided and all by herself.

And now she must face it all unaided, and all by herself. There was no one she could shuffle this burden on to. Life only went forward, never back. And even when you took the wrong turning, and watched yourself sailing towards the darkness, wide-eyed, you had no option but sail on or sink . . .

CHAPTER EIGHT

THE WINTER deepened.

Not that she'd noticed. Romy had been too wrapped up in her own private world of bitterness to care about the changing season.

This was not an English winter of leafless trees and icy winds, but it was a lowest ebb in nature, all the same. The countryside had turned predominantly brown, and though the skies were almost always blue it was a cold, clear blue without warmth. And the mountains all around were now filigreed and inlaid with seams of white snow.

It was winter in the house, too.

Over the past week, Xavier's face had changed no more than the granite mountains had done. And it had remained just as cold.

That slight frowning at the dark eyebrows, expressing nothing more than the concentration of a powerful mind; that tightness at the mouth, as though biting back any expression; that bleakness in the cold grey eyes—these were what she had seen, morning and night, day after day, for a whole empty week. An indifference that was as fixed as the cast of a bronze mask. At the dining-table, where she sat opposite her husband, hardly ever exchanging more than polite formalities with him.

Whenever they had guests, he treated her courteously, attentively even, but always as though she herself were another guest, rather than as a wife. Neither unkind nor ardent, neither hostile nor warm.

And when they were alone together, he behaved as though she were not there at all, making no effort to bring her out of her silence, nor uttering a word of comment about her inertia.

It was as though her feelings had ceased to matter to him any more. As though he had given up with her.

And she felt that she herself no longer cared.

Oh, yes, the frantic sensation of being trapped, which had been so unbearable when she'd first learned the truth from Xavier, had lost its edge. Except that the resignation that had followed was in some ways worse.

She never did make that call home. It was pointless talking to Laura, or with any of her family, about Xavier. They simply couldn't understand how things stood between her and him. To really understand, you would have had to have been there, in the Athenaeum that morning. Or to have seen his face on their wedding night.

There was no sense in trying to make them understand. As the days passed, she realised that she didn't *want* them to know how things really stood between her and Xavier. She certainly didn't want Papa to feel that he'd made a terrible mistake. Teo, she knew, was harder and more selfish. The firm meant a great deal to him, and he'd had few qualms in matching her with Xavier. But Papa had acted out of nothing more than love for her. She'd already said too much. She must not confide in Laura any further.

Bitterness had settled into her, like a gall in the living wood of a tree. A hard lump of acrid resentment that had enclosed her heart, and that was always there.

Xavier, at least, had his work.

How she envied him that! Every morning and most afternoons, he was immersed in the mechanics of livestock to be bought and sold, of agricultural machines and chemicals to be stocked, of this year's vintage to be bottled, of next year's vintage to be prepared for.

And while he worked she was faced with the impossible

task of amusing herself.

There was no shortage of female company for her, of course. Already she had made several acquaintances among the wives and daughters of Xavier's friends; no one she could call a true friend yet, but plenty of amusing companions with whom she could share the empty hours.

They tended to be rich women, whose chosen haunts were the scented, rustling purlieus of expensive boutiques. All were a great deal more experienced at spending large sums of money than Romy. But it was not a skill that Romy felt she wanted to pick up.

She could not share their quintessentially Italian delight in silver, silk, scented leather and costly clothes. The amount of antique silver boxes, exquisite dresses, and mind-bogglingly expensive handbags that they could buy in one afternoon's shopping in Palermo was a lesson in extravagance.

'You're so frugal,' she had been told more than once, and it was unmistakably an accusation. 'Xavier is a generous man. What about these darling ear-rings? They would suit you to perfection, *cara*!'

But Romy had declined the darling ear-rings with their telephone-number price tag. Though Xavier had given Romy a cheque-book with apparently fathomless reserves under its lizard-skin covers, she had no taste for such conspicuous and empty spending. It amused her to watch others revelling in clothes or jewels, but she had little enthusiasm for such material pleasures. She could not live on shopping, novels and chocolate.

Her mind was far too occupied with thoughts of Xavier. He, too, had no shortage of friends. The telephone never seemed to stop ringing in their house—calls from Paris or Frankfurt or New York.

Friendship or business? She didn't always know, because Xavier slipped into French or German with complete assurance, and she couldn't follow. Sometimes the conversations were about dollars or deutschmarks, sometimes about mutual friends. And sometimes she heard Xavier's husky laughter, and knew in her heart that he was talking to a woman. On those occasions, she was tormented by the suspicion that the woman at the other end of the line was Eva.

'I will raise no objections if you keep a mistress. Or any number of mistresses, as you please.' Had she really once said that?

On the occasions when he was away, usually for no more than two days at a time, she was especially depressed. She knew that travelling was an important part of his work, yet she could not lay the ghost of her unhappiness to rest. The thought that he might be with other women was horrible and, shut it out though she might, it always returned to haunt her.

She slept alone every night in the crimson bedroom, unforgiven and unwanted. Xavier no longer came there, and some nights she lay awake for hours on end, neither needing nor wanting sleep. Humiliating as it was to admit it, she missed him most in bed.

The absence of Xavier's lovemaking was a huge void in her life. As far as their physical relationship went, it had been nothing short of sensational. She had found herself responding to him whether she wanted to or not, her body defying her mind in the exquisite sublimation of a kind of sex she had never imagined could exist.

It had been a developing passion that had become almost overwhelmingly intense, their encounters seeking more deliberate avenues of pleasure, prolonging the ecstasy until sometimes she'd thought her heart would burst . . .

She had to tear her thoughts away from the memories, when they came, because they made her existence all the more wearisomely empty.

The festivities of Christmas came and went with no sign of a reconciliation. They exchanged expensive gifts, but not one pennyworth of warmth was given on either side.

On New Year's Eve they held a huge and glittering party which lasted well until the dawn. She danced and laughed, and played the dazzling *baronessa* to perfection. But inwardly Romy sensed no lifting of her heart. All she felt was a sharpened awareness of how empty her life had become. When the last of the guests had departed, she and Xavier went their separate ways, to their separate lives.

Early in January, Xavier told her that two foals had been born on the estate, and invited her to come and see them. Her dulled interest aroused, she went with him through a crisp covering of frost to the stable-yard. It was the first non-social thing they'd done together for a long time.

The foals were in the most sheltered of the stables, which was heated by a massive wood-burning stove at this time of year.

Gangling, clumsy things, their gentle charm went straight to Romy's heart. One was suckling its mother's milk, while the other, more inquisitive, had come stumbling over to Romy, with a mixture of friendliness and shy readiness to bolt.

She reached out to touch the young creature, aware of a lump growing in her throat. If she and Xavier had still been sleeping together, she might by now be pregnant. The thought was both painful and sweet at the same time. It was not easy to explain her feelings.

'They're so beautiful,' she whispered, stroking the glossy coat of the foal. The mother's trusting eyes rolled quietly at her.

'They should be good horses.' Xavier nodded. 'The sire is magnificent, and both mothers are good mounts. Do you want to name them?' The bulky sheepskin jacket he wore suited him to perfection; the upturned collar made a rugged frame for his dark face.

'I'll have to think,' she said. 'I'm not very good at names.'

'You'll have plenty of time to think about it,' he said casually. 'They're yours.'

'Mine?'

'Both of them.' He smiled slightly. 'Starting now. When they get older, you can break them to the saddle yourself. That way, they'll be completely yours.'

Romy, lost for words, just stroked the nuzzling mouth of the foal. 'You're very generous,' she said at last, in a strained voice. Her feelings weren't altogether without irony. 'Not many men would make such a gift, off the cuff.'

'Off the cuff?' he repeated. 'What makes you think this was off the cuff?'

'Well, it can't have been planned!'

He walked to the little office at the end of the stables, and returned with the stock ledger, a heavy volume bound in black leather. Folding it open, he passed it silently to her.

Romy straightened as she hefted the tome, and looked at the entries. The page was dated April of the previous year. The record of the two matings was there, with subsequent veterinary notes confirming that both mares had conceived.

What caught her eye were the initials which appeared in the space marked 'Owner': *R.J.F.* Her own initials.

'I don't understand,' she said, looking up at him.

'They were planned for you,' he said gently. 'Two, in case one went wrong. I wanted them to be born especially for you.'

'You planned them for *me?* Nine months ago?' she said, her eyes widening.

'I told you before,' Xavier shrugged. 'I had an elaborate courtship planned. More fool me.' He took the stock ledger back from her nerveless fingers. 'In any case, they are yours now. Enjoy them.'

'Oh, Xavier,' she whispered, her eyes filling with tears, 'they're absolutely wonderful. Nothing like this has ever happened to me. I just don't know what to say. Thank you sounds so lame for a gift like this, but it's all I have. Thank you.'

His grey eyes glittered for a moment. 'I'm glad you like them.' He nodded without smiling.

Too choked with emotion to say anything more, Romy slipped her arms round the foal's slender neck, and pressed her face to the sweet-smelling skin. Of all the gifts he could have made her, nothing could have touched her more than this. Sometimes he did things that took her breath away and left her gasping, all her preconceptions about him overturned.

Generosity like this was just unbelievable. Yet it was an intrinsic part of Xavier's nature; just as his harshness and his refusal to let her go were also a part of him. He confused her more than any other person she'd ever known.

She was so involved with the foals that Xavier eventually had to point out that the mothers were getting restless at their continued presence. 'You'll have plenty of time to get to know them,' he reminded her. 'For today, it's best to leave them with the mares. You can come and see them again in another couple of days.'

When they finally emerged from the stables, an hour later, the sun had momentarily come out. The spaniels, prohibited from coming in with the foals, greeted them joyously. As though understanding that she wasn't ready to go back to the house, Xavier turned to her. 'It isn't too cold for a walk. Why don't we take a stroll in the woods before we drive back?'

She nodded her acceptance. The dogs came bounding eagerly in their wake, yapping excitedly at the prospect of a walk.

The wind was brisk and slightly cutting. Walking a little way apart from Xavier, she let him guide her up through the rocky hillside towards the woods. The crenellated leaves of the oaks had turned to rustling brown paper, but still clung obstinately to the branches. They would not fall until the new leaves pushed them off in the spring; in the meantime, they let the light come through, and the grassy turf under the trees was sprinkled with winter flowers, crocuses and creamy hellebores, and little pink stars that had no name, or no name that Romy knew.

Huddled into her jacket, Romy was aware of an emotion burning in her. Shame. It was bewildering to realise that he'd been thinking so tenderly about her all those months ago. Planning such a magnificent gift, especially for her. Spending not just money, but time and imagination, in order to do this, to thrill her to her core. Glimpses like that of his real nature made her feel utterly wretched, made her wonder whether she really understood him at all. Whether, as Xavier had once accused her, her heart had been padlocked, and the key mislaid for ever.

It was terrible to think that her emotions were growing warped and sterile, that time was passing by, and her life wasting. With a sharp pang, she felt that she must straighten herself out, as simple as that, or face the consequences, consequences that might include losing her husband—if she had not already lost him.

It was up to her. If she wanted this marriage to work, then she had to play her part of the game. Submit to his will, in other words. Be his lover in bed, and bear his children when the time came. Love, honour and obey. Become the yielding, submissive wife he had always wanted her to be.

But, even if she could reconcile herself to that capitulation, would her first, uncertain step be rejected? Would she find those iron doors crashing shut in her face, all over again? She felt that she couldn't bear another rejection from Xavier. Not now.

'What are you thinking?' he asked, his eyes on her face.

'About you, and the things you do. I don't understand you, Xavier. You're not like anyone I've ever met in my life!'

'I should hope not,' he commented.

She turned to him, her mouth as pale pink and tender as a rose-petal bruised by rain. 'I didn't know—I never guessed that you'd had things like this planned.'

'You knew I wanted to marry you two years ago,' he reminded her evenly. 'Why should it surprise you that I made plans for your amusement?'

'Perhaps it shouldn't. But I'm glad you were still . . . interested . . . enough in me to carry out your original intention.'

'Interested?' he repeated coolly. 'Who else do I have to give the foals to now? I planned them for you. There was no reason why you should not have them.'

'It was still kind of you. I just wanted you to know that I . . . appreciated that kindness.

He shrugged slightly. 'Am I not always kind to you?'

'There are many different sorts of kindness,' Romy replied. 'You are kind in some ways, cruel in others.'

'Really?' He lifted one eyebrow. 'Give me an example of how I have been cruel to you?'

'You—you told me you felt nothing but indifference for me,' she reminded him, the colour leaving her face. 'You said you were detached from me. That was cruel of you.' She was breaking the unwritten rules, disobeying the unspoken conventions that had governed their cold, silent existence together for weeks past. Xavier was watching her with exactly the smiling, handsome mask that most infuriated her. 'Do you find this conversation amusing?' she demanded.

'There is a certain irony,' he said drily. 'As I remember it, *you* were the one who found me unacceptable as a husband. Are you suddenly becoming the loving little wife again, because I've given you two horses?'

'I'm not becoming anything. But I wanted to explain the way I reacted that day.' She didn't have to explain what day. They both knew what she was talking about. 'The truth came as a shock to me, Xavier. I'm glad you told me, now. I've been incredibly naïve about it all, and it was a relief to have some of my nightmares demolished.' She glanced at him. 'After all, it was horrible to feel that I'd been bought and paid for. Now I know that it wasn't like that. And I've misjudged you about the shares.' She hung her head for a moment. 'It was very generous of you to lend Papa that money. More than generous. You've been a good friend to my family.'

Xavier turned to whistle for the dogs, then met her troubled eyes. 'Is there any more?' he asked casually.

His coldness to her was hurtful, but she went on. 'I felt betrayed, Xavier. I wish you could understand that. I felt that you'd tricked me in a horrible way. It was like—like finding yourself imprisoned on a life sentence for something you'd never done.'

'A very pretty speech.' He was standing facing her, his eyes narrowed. 'And now?'

'I still feel that we've been thrust together for all the wrong reasons,' she said in a low voice. 'Maybe I'm too rebellious, but I had certain illusions about the man I would marry, and the way I would choose him.' She raised her eyes to his. 'You were chosen for me. It was all so . . . so mechanical. We didn't marry because we loved each other, but because it was financially desirable. There just wasn't enough emotion in it . . .'

'Not on your side, perhaps,' he said obliquely. 'Is there a point to all this, Romy?'

'The point is just . . .' She braced herself. 'We haven't exchanged more than pleasantries since before Christmas. We haven't smiled at each other or slept together . . . Do you still feel nothing . . . but indifference?'

Her voice had tailed off almost to a whisper, and she dared not look up at his face.

His laughter was unmistakably mocking. 'I see. The usual female vanity. You want to know whether, after such a long absence from your bed, I am not consumed with lust for your fair body?'

'That wasn't what I meant,' she said, colouring angrily.

'Wasn't it? I think it was.' His eyes slid down her figure with slow consideration. 'The answer is that you are still as desirable to me as you ever were.' The deep, husky voice made her shiver, touching some nerve deep inside her. He smiled smokily. 'I would make love to you here and now, under these trees, if I thought you had any inclination for the pleasure.'

'But I haven't,' she said shakily, breathing more quickly now. 'I haven't the slightest inclination for the *pleasure*, as you call it.' Her eyes were as cold as the wind. 'You're being deliberately insulting!'

'So are you,' he replied. 'But of course, you won't let me near you until there's no danger of conception, will you?'

She turned away. It was no use. There could be no reconciliation. Too much had been said between them.

'Come on,' he said brusquely, taking her arm. 'It's getting cold. There is no sense our staying out here, tormenting each other.' She pulled away from him, and they turned to walk back to the car.

The hurt was intense, spreading up through her heart, and tears of frustration sprang to her eyes, squeezing between her lids. He didn't care for her any more. She had destroyed his feelings for her. The feeling of failure, of helplessness, was almost unbearable.

The world was blurred around her. She felt so utterly lonely, so cut off from him, that she could do nothing, nothing at all. Today it had seemed that she had had a chance to settle their differences, to reach out to Xavier and start anew. And this chance, too, had been dashed. Would there ever be another?

In the succeeding days, the foals found a special place in the aching void of her heart. She preferred their company to that of people, at present. It was better to be with them than to be caught up in the bright chatter and social life of her friends.

Whenever she could, she made time to go out to the stables and be with them. Watching them grow was something she could not tire of. With uncanny speed, they had changed from awkward, stumbling things to proud little gambollers, able to trot and frisk with the grace of their breed. Still shy and unsure with humans, she received a deep pleasure in trying to tame them, to tempt them over to her with sugar or carrots.

She found names for them: Florio and Ebony. Rather grandiose at present, but they would soon grow into them. She made friends with the vet, a man in his late fifties, and tried to be on hand whenever he came to check them over.

'Stroke them all you want to,' he urged her. 'As long as you're quiet and gentle with them, it can only do them good to get used to being handled. You could even start leading them if you like.'

'It isn't too soon?'

'Not if you're sensible, and stay close to the mares. Get someone to slip the halter on for you while you gentle them.'

So she started putting the halter on the foals, alternately, and leading them briefly around the yard outside the stable. She also started training them to let her pick up their feet and examine their hooves. The slow process of teaching them to have confidence in her was some consolation for the cold emptiness of her life.

Xavier made no comment about her new interest, but she guessed he was pleased that his gift had meant so much to her, and that she had found something to occupy her mind with.

'Florio's my favourite,' she told him.

'Why?'

'He's by far the more difficult to tame of the two. Ebony's lovely, but Florio has a streak of the devil in him. He never does what you want, and he needs so much more attention.'

'You must feel an affinity, then,' he commented drily.

It was that very affinity with the foal that enabled her to tell instantly when something started to go wrong with Florio.

When she'd gone to the stables that morning, the bay foal had been restless, and had refused to let her touch him. She'd thought he felt slightly sweaty, too. After she'd watched him for a while, the foal had seemed to settle down, but the feeling of disquiet had remained with her.

She ate lunch alone. Xavier had been away for two days. He was in Rome on business, and wasn't due back until tomorrow night. Without him, the house felt empty and strange. She longed to be able to discuss the foal with him. She thought of ringing him in Rome, but dismissed the idea. She would only get a snub.

When she went back to take another look at Florio after lunch, her heart sank. The foal was definitely sweating now. His coat was dark and wet. Worse, he was clearly in pain, grunting and trying to bite at his belly. The word 'colic' formed ominously in her mind.

She ran to the office, and rang the vet at once.

'Try and walk him, even if he kicks,' the vet ordered. 'I'll be over as soon as I can.'

Romy was taut with anxiety as she stuggled to lead Florio out of the stables. He was kicking and twisting now, and his strength was incredible for such a young animal. His skin was fiery-hot, and his breathing was hoarse. The way his eyes were rolling terrified her.

'Let me take him, *signora*,' one of the stable-hands urged. 'He will hurt you.'

'I'm all right.' She'd already had two painful kicks from the panicky animal, but she knew that Florio trusted no one as much as he trusted her. She part coaxed, part dragged him into a walk, trying to avoid the flailing, though luckily as yet unshod, hooves. He was still shaking his head up and down, acting as though something were attacking him from underneath. If only Xavier were here! Of all the unlucky times for him to be away. She'd never missed his calm strength so much as now.

She gasped as Florio reared back, hauling on the leader, and tried to pull his head back down. But the foal was too much in pain to obey. His one intention was to get down on to the ground, and roll away the pain that was twisting his guts.

Helplessly, Romy sank to her knees as Florio lay in the cobbled yard and screamed, rolling his slender body until the ribs showed under his wet coat like full-drawn longbows. Her eyes were flooded with tears. But she had to have strength.

'Help me get him back on his feet,' she commanded the men around her. 'He has to keep walking until the vet gets here.'

Willing hands helped her raise the stricken foal, and joined her in leading him round and round. From inside the stables, she could hear Florio's mother whinnying, and the frantic drumming of her hooves against the kick board. They set off at an uneven pace, round and round, round and round. A thin, sleety rain began to fall.

Filthy and exhausted, she sank down in the hallway, and closed her eyes. It was evening. Her arms ached, but they were nothing to the pain in her legs, where the foal's sharp hooves had kicked her. One leg of her jeans was stained with her own blood. She was also soaked with the freezing rain that was now falling heavily. Yet she was numb inside.

'*Signora!*' Clucking with horror, the servants fluttered round her. Concetta, more sensible than the rest, had run for a glass of something strong. Romy gulped at the dark liquid. As the taste of the Marsala filled her mouth, her mind was flooded with memories.

Memories of how she had sat in this same hallway, months ago, and had drank Marsala on her wedding night. Then, too, she had been exhausted and filled with pain. Then, too, despair had washed her soul.

Florio was dying. Her diagnosis of colic had been accurate, and lethal in the case of such a young foal. The vet had been with him for hours, but the foal was in the last stages of exhaustion by now, unable to even walk any more. As his breathing had grown shallow and rapid, and his tongue had lolled out, she'd been unable to bear it.

Watching him die was too much like watching the destruction of her own happiness, her own hopes. As though the foal were a symbol of what might have been, of the promise that had failed so tragically.

She desperately needed to speak to Xavier. Waving away help, she rose and walked on stiff legs to the study. She knew the people Xavier would probably be staying with in Rome; they had been at Luca for Christmas, and he usually stayed with them when he went to the capital. As soon as she'd found their number in the telephone book, she rang them.

But the woman who answered sounded surprised. 'Xavier? He is not here, Romy. What made you think he would be in Rome?'

'He said he was going on business,' she said in confusion. 'I assumed he'd be with you——'

'We sorted all our business out over Christmas,' came the reply. 'There's nothing to discuss at present. He may well be in Rome right now, of course, but he's not staying with us. Do you want me to telephone the Scalabrinis to see if he is there?'

'N-no, I'll do that myself, thanks.' Feeling like a fool, she thanked the other woman, and rang off.

But Xavier wasn't at the Scalabrinis, either. And he'd said nothing to them about coming to Rome.

Her heart was thudding heavily as she rang off a second time. There was a quicker way to find out whether Xavier had flown to Rome or not.

It took only a brief call to Alitalia to discover that he had not. Had not been on any flight to Rome, and was not booked on any flight back from Rome.

She sat in the study, staring ahead of her with sightless

eyes. She'd always had her suspicions. How ironic that they should be coming true now, while Florio lay dying in the stables.

She walked into the hall, meeting the housekeeper there. 'I want to speak to the chauffeur,' she ordered with icy control. 'Would you call him for me, please?'

'At once, *signora*.'

She waited where she stood, rigid as a board. The chauffeur, out of uniform, came hurrying in a few minutes later.

'*Signora?* Does the *signora* want the car?'

'No,' Romy said shortly. 'I want to know where you took my husband two days ago.'

The man's face was at first surprised, then nervous. 'To the airport, *signora*. To get the flight to Rome.'

'You're lying.'

'No, *signora*! As God is my witness——'

Romy's eyes blazed at him. 'Don't lie to me, Gesualdo. I'm not a fool. You didn't take him to the airport, and he didn't get the flight to Rome.' Tangled-haired and white-faced as she was, the man actually quailed before her anger. 'Now tell me. Where *did* you take him?'

Gesualdo gulped. 'To the *signora's*. The other *signora*.'

'What the hell are you talking about?' she flared, her nerves tight.

'I took the master to Signora Eva's villa, at Lipari,' he said, trying to smile.

'To Eva's?' She felt a wave of nausea. 'Is that where you left him?'

'Yes, *signora*.'

'And that's where you're going to pick him up again?'

Gesualdo's brow was shining now. 'Tomorrow afternoon, at the railway station at Lipari. That is what he commanded, *Baronessa*. He did not wish you to know——'

'Get out,' Romy whispered, and the man fled.

She walked blindly up the stairs, trying to shut out the images that clamoured at her brain. While she'd been here, trusting and alone, Xavier had been with Eva. A three-day sojourn in the yellow villa at Lipari, in the arms of a woman who did not refuse him her favours, and whom he had always desired.

She'd refused to sleep with him. Well, there was no shortage of willing women to take her place. He could prove that any time he wanted to.

But that he'd chosen Eva was so utterly cruel that it made her dizzy.

Until her thoughts went one step further.

The more she thought about it, the more logical it got. It all added up. Perhaps his visit to Eva was not a casual decision, after all. Perhaps he'd never had any intention whatsoever of stopping his affair with her. There was logic in that, too.

A handsome couple who had been happy and loving, but childless. A first marriage that had been annulled, but had never really broken down. A second wife, brought in from abroad, with no affection to tie her to her husband . . .

She clenched her teeth at the picture her thoughts had conjured up. It chilled her in a way that the winter cold had not done. Roma Forlari had been brought here for no other reason than to provide breeding stock, to bear legitimate heirs to the baron's aristocratic line. That first marriage was clearly still alive, in practice if not in name. And when she had refused to let him make love to her there had been no urgency.

Using the lever of the money, he could afford to keep her here, waiting until she came round. And in the meantime he could amuse himself with the woman he had always preferred above all others . . .

She hunted through her drawers for some money, her

mind numbed and bruised beyond endurance. Xavier
had hurt her once too often. She was not going to spend
another night in this house. She would drive straight to
Catania, to the airport. If there wasn't a flight to London
tonight, she would spend the night in a hotel, and get the
first flight available tomorrow.

She was crying as she stripped off her filthy clothes and
changed into clean jeans and a jacket. Trying to restore
some semblance of order to her image in the glass was
well-nigh impossible. The face that stared back at her was
wild-haired, distraught, its cheeks streaked with tears.

It was over. The disaster that had been her marriage
had finally come to an end. She would never see Xavier
again.'

She threw some clothes into an overnight bag, forced
herself to stop crying, and went downstairs. A frightened
servant was waiting for her.

'*Signora*? Do you want some dinner now?'

'I won't be staying for dinner. 'I'm going . . . away.'

'*Signora*——'

'When your master gets back,' Romy added, turning
at the door, 'tell him——' She paused, her mind empty,
then shrugged painfully. 'Tell him nothing.'

'*Signora!*'

But Romy was already outside, the keys of the Range
Rover in her hand. She climbed into the big car, started it
up, and drove away from the house. The rain puddled the
windscreen, the slashing wipers hardly able to cope with
the downpour. The gravelled road was squelchy beneath
her wheels, and she drove fast, with the blind purpose of
intense grief.

How could he have done this to her? How *could* he?
What crime had she ever committed that warranted this?
What had she ever done to him that would justify such a
betrayal?

She had loved him so deeply. Yes, she had loved him. There was no sense in denying it to herself any more. Xavier had become her world, her everything. She'd only been living through him these past months. She knew with sudden grief that she could never love another man the way she had loved Xavier.

Telling herself she hated him was only a blind for her real feelings. She'd thought there was no more to understand. She'd thought that she and Xavier had nothing whatsoever in common. How did you ever learn to understand everything, to untie all the emotional knots and tangles that lay hidden within yourself? Sometimes you didn't even know they were there until they tripped you up, and sent you sprawling on your face . . .

She was already on the road to Catania when the thought burst into her mind. *Florio.*

In her passionate hurt and anger over Xavier and Eva, she'd forgotten the little foal completely. He might even now be dead. But she knew she couldn't go without knowing his fate. She had loved him, too, in her way, and she owed him that.

Without thinking any further, she slammed the brakes on, pulled off the road, and swung the Range Rover round to head back to Luca.

She didn't even see the truck, didn't even bother to look the other way.

All she saw, at the last minute, was the blaze of headlights bearing down on her. It was too quick for her to feel fear, only a pang of regret that this was the way it was going to end. The horrified braying of a klaxon invaded her mind.

And then the impact, too huge to comprehend, lifting the Range Rover bodily and dragging it down the road, a long, long way, among an inferno of noise and motion.

And then, blackness.

CHAPTER NINE

THE UNRELIEVED night of anaesthesia blended into a chiaroscuro of dreams and distant noises. Romy knew she was in hospital. She had a memory, some time after the crash, of having been taken there, of a succession of dazzling lights flitting overhead as she was wheeled down a corridor. Also of a bright room where faces came and went over her, where the familiar, ominous smells of medicines were sharp in her nostrils.

She wasn't dead. That was surprising.

As a kind of consciousness returned, she became aware that she was in a small private ward. A drip had been inserted into her arm, and it must have contained some pain-killing drug, because she was completely without pain.

Without physical pain, that was; the memory was there, somewhere at the back of her mind, of what had happened. She felt a kind of numbed disbelief. Why? Why had he done it? Deliberately, she let other images invade her thoughts, snapshots of sunny days in the past, nostalgic clips from the archive of her memory. Green fields starred with flowers. Her mother, walking with her across the downs, her long, ash-blonde hair floating in the wind. A foal, cantering gaily at the end of a halter . . .

She drifted off to sleep again.

When Romy woke for the second time, it was sharply, to full wakefulness. The curtains were half-drawn, and the bright sunlight of a winter's afternoon poured into the little room. There was a smell of flowers. Lilies.

She knew at once who had put them there. She turned her head on the pillow, and met Xavier's grey eyes. He had been sitting beside her, watching her. Again, as once before, she felt that strange certainty that he had been waiting not for hours, but for years.

He rose from his chair, took a glass off her bedside cabinet and raised it to her lips. Her mouth was so dry that the barley-water seemed to sink in before she had time to swallow it; but at least her tongue was now moist enough for her to be able to whisper.

'The other driver?'

'Not even a scratch.'

'Thank heaven.'

'He was high enough in his cab to escape any injury. But he's had a bad fright.'

Romy closed her eyes again, relief sharp and clean in her. 'It was my fault.'

'Drink some more. You're dehydrated.' His firm hand lifted her head forward, and she gulped painfully at the liquid. Swallowing told her that her throat was fiery and tender, and one side of her body was turning into a vast, dismal ache.

She opened her eyes dully. Her left arm and shoulder were encased in bandages, only her fingers protruding from the end of the tube. Several nails were broken, but when she made an attempt to stir them the pale pink fingers moved obediently. The effort made her gasp with pain, though.

She lifted a shaky right hand to wipe her face. Something else had occurred to her. 'Florio?'

Xavier put the glass down. 'Like you, he survived. He's trotting around as though nothing had happened.'

She looked directly at him for the first time. There were stark lines of fatigue in his face, and a black stubble of beard covered his cheeks and chin. But his eyes were as clear and cold as the hospital steel, and his voice was calm. 'Don't you want to know what the damage to *you* is?'

'You'll tell me, when you feel like it.'

'A fractured humerus. Two fractures of the radius. Suspected fracture of the hip. Multiple contusions.' Muscles knotted along his jaw. 'You've just performed a minor miracle, Romy. There was hardly room inside the Range Rover for a cat, let alone an adult human being. That truck just trampled it into the road.

'I feel trampled.' Her mouth twisted in a bitter smile. She rolled her head on the pillow. 'Why are you here, Xavier? Do you really think I want to see you at this moment?'

He was silent for a short while. When he spoke again, his voice was deeper, rougher. 'I know what you found out last night, Romy. And I know what you imagined.'

'You mean the truth about you?' His presence here was hurting her more than the broken arm. 'Please, Xavier. Leave me alone. For once in my life, have some respect for my wishes, and just go away.'

'You're confused,' he said gently.

'Not any more,' she snapped back fiercely. 'I was confused when I still thought there was a grain of humanity or kindness in you. But I see things clearly now, very clearly indeed!' She tried to sit up in bed, but the pain was too great. 'Just tell me one thing,' she blazed at him. 'How many of those *business trips* were visits to dear Eva? Were you cheating on me right from the start, or did you decide to go back to her once we stopped sleeping together——'

He laid a gentle hand on her lips. 'Romy, stop. It has been a long, long time since there was anything more than the merest friendship between me and Eva.'

'And what were you doing while you stayed at her villa for three days?' she asked with biting irony. 'Playing a friendly game of contract bridge?'

'I have not been at Eva's,' he replied quietly. 'I've been in Rome.'

'Such a crude lie?' she said contemptuously, sinking back against the pillows. 'You must think the accident has turned me into an idiot!'

'It's the truth.' His eyes burned into hers. 'Yes, I asked Gesualdo to take me to Lipari. Eva needed to see me. But I was only there for a few hours. Then I left for Rome. You don't know this, Romy, but since the divorce I've continued to run my ex-wife's financial affairs. She has very little conception of how to handle money. It can't have escaped your attention,' he said drily, 'that Eva is not exactly an intellectual giant.'

'She has enough brains to know what she wants,' Romy said icily.

'But not enough to take care of her own money,' he answered. 'I could not avoid a sense of responsibility for her, Romy. She is congenitally unable to look after her own finances, and she is a wealthy woman in her own right. Her own family in Germany used to run her affairs, but her father is dead now. I've been running her investments for years. That is why she came to see me that afternoon when you met her at Luca. To discuss some business to do with her estate.'

'Touching devotion on your part,' Romy said wearily, turning her face away from him in disbelief. 'I'd like to be alone now, Xavier.'

'Listen to me,' he said harshly. 'I'm telling you the truth, Romy. I went to Lipari to see her for a very particular reason.'

'*Very* particular,' she echoed bitterly.

'The purpose of my visit was to hand over all the information about her property to her new accountant. When I married you, I knew that I could no longer act as Eva's financial advisor. As a divorced couple, there had been nothing wrong with it. Now that I had another wife, it was something that had to come to an end.'

'Your ethics are remarkable,' she put in.

Xavier went on, ignoring her sarcasm. 'I told her that she

would have to employ a proper accountant from now on. As usual, it's taken her a couple of months to mobilise herself, but she has finally engaged a reputable international firm in Palermo. The reason I went to her villa two days ago was to meet the new man, to pass on all the bonds and certificates which I had been keeping in the safe at our house, and to give him the full portfolio of the investments I'd made on Eva's behalf. She,' he added, 'wouldn't have the faintest idea where her own money was. She doesn't even know what she's worth. She is the sort of woman who has always depended on men to run her life for her.'

Romy was staring at him silently now, her pale face taut. 'This is a very complicated story,' she said slowly.

'The truth usually is.' He leaned forward, dark brows emphasizing the brilliance of his grey eyes. 'Let me tell you something, Romy. I really am not all that friendly with Eva. She hurt me badly, and I long ago lost my respect for her. But I had the idea that if I showed obvious affection for my ex-wife, it would move you to jealousy.'

Romy grimaced. 'Of course it stirred me to jealousy!'

'I know. It was a foolish idea, and once I'd seen how much you'd been hurt by it, I decided not to repeat the experiment. That was why I hid that last visit from you. That was stupid of me. But when I considered the state our relationship was in, I felt that you just didn't need to know that I was going to see Eva, or that I'd been taking care of Eva's money all this time. It was simpler to not tell you.'

'It's always been simpler to lie to me,' Romy said shakily, 'right from the very beginning. Hasn't it?'

'No,' he answered in a quiet voice. It would have been simpler to tell you the truth, right from the beginning. Simpler, and better. I will never lie to you again, Romy. Not about anyone or anything.'

In the silence that followed, the distant noises of the hospital seeped in through the half-open door. A nurse peeped into the room and, seeing that Romy was awake, went off to fetch a doctor.

Her arm, side and hip were throbbing painfully now, but she could not take her eyes off Xavier. The possibility that she had been wrong was devastating. 'So what did you do for the rest of the three days?' she asked, her voice hovering between challenge and plea.

'I took the express train from Lipari to Rome that night,' he replied calmly. 'The sleeper. I like the night-train. It's less tiring than flying. By the next morning I was in Rome. I stayed at the Imperial, near the Borghese gardens, which is one of my favourite hotels in the world.' He reached into his pocket. 'I've got the bill, if you want to see it.'

'Give it to me,' she said huskily.

He passed her the piece of paper, and she unfolded it awkwardly with her good hand. As she studied it numbly, he went on in the same calm voice. 'I had meetings with various people I needed to see. I should have telephoned you at least once, but I wasn't in the mood. I bitterly regret that now. It was only one of many, many occasions when a little kindness on my part would have saved a lot of anguish. But,' he said heavily, 'I was angry with you.'

'Go on.'

'There's little more to tell you. I got my business done, and had lunch with an old schoolfriend. A *male* schoolfriend. Then I prepared to return to Sicily. I had asked Gesualdo to meet me at Lipari station. That simply happens to be the nearest stop to Luca.'

The hotel bill was incontrovertible. He'd stayed there for two nights, and it was all listed in black and white, down to the coffee he'd ordered before leaving last night. He'd checked out at ten o'clock. She looked up at him, her eyes starting to fill with tears.

'They telephoned me at the hotel last night to tell me what had happened,' he said, and his handsome face tightened at the memory. 'All the servants knew was that there had been a terrible accident, and that you'd been taken to hospital, unconscious and covered in blood. I took the first flight I could get back to Sicily, in a private plane. I didn't find out exactly what had happened to you until the early hours of this morning, when I got to the hospital.'

Her voice was barely audible. 'Were you worried?'

'Worried?' His expression was incredulous. 'You still don't understand, do you? I was gutted, Romy. I will never forget last night, I can promise you that.'

She only had to look at his face to know that he was telling her the truth. He had suffered. The marks of strain and tension were as clear on his face as if they'd been written there. The tracks left by emotion, real emotion, emotion that had her as its centre. He cared about her, more deeply and truly than she'd ever wanted to believe.

'Oh, Xavier.' Hot tears spilled down her cheeks helplessly. 'I've made such a bloody awful mess of everything . . .'

'Hush,' he commanded, his expression gentling at the sight of her grief.

'You must hate me,' she said hopelessly, as he dried her cheeks.

'No,' he replied in a soft voice. 'I don't hate you, Romy. That's foolish.'

'Then you must wonder whether we'll ever have a normal marriage!'

'Normal?' he repeated. 'If I'd wanted normality, I'd have married someone else.'

'You should have done,' she said sadly. 'Why *did* you choose me? You've given yourself so much trouble and misery since we married!'

'Believe it or not, it's all been worth it.' He smiled crookedly. 'I could never have loved someone ordinary, someone incapable of depths or heights.' He looked into her eyes. 'I married you because I wanted a special marriage, Romy. Because you're special, the most special woman I've ever known.'

She couldn't help the question spilling out. 'And Eva? Don't you love her?'

His sudden smile was like a shaft of sunlight. 'What is this?' he asked, stroking her hair gently. 'A fit of insecurity? Don't you believe what I've just been telling you?'

'I imagine you had more fun with her than you're having with me,' she added with a touch of bitter humour. 'You obviously care about her. You must have loved her.'

For a while, he was silent, as though searching for the words in his mind. 'If you want the truth,' he said at last, 'I once thought I loved her, yes. Remember, though, that I was only twenty-five years old when I first married. Remember how much time has passed since then, how many years ago it was. We were both young and careless. Pleasure and gaiety were what seemed to matter most then. My relationship with Eva was primarily youthful. I don't think I'm being unkind to her when I say it was also immature.'

'Is that meant to soothe my jealousy?' she asked drily, looking up at him from the pillow.

'It's the truth. It was a shallow marriage. A marriage between heedless, rather spoiled young people. We'd grown up together, you see, and it was always expected that we would marry. But we were both mistaken in the other, and finding out the truth was something of a shock for both of us. We just weren't suited, Romy, either in bed or out of it. It was Eva who wanted her freedom.' He grimaced. 'She'd already had an affair or two by then. But although I knew in my heart that there ought to be more to marriage than what Eva and I had, I kept my vows up to the last. If I appear to you a libertine now, then remember this—that I never betrayed my wife.' Xavier met her eyes seriously. 'And if you think divorce was easy, or that I undertook it lightly, you're very much mistaken. It was a very traumatic period, which did a great deal to turn me from a youth into a mature man.' He lifted her good hand to his lips, unexpectedly, and kissed her palm. His lips were warm, her fingers brushing the masculine roughness of his jawline. 'Five years have passed since the divorce,' he said, his eyes on hers. 'And I am a lot wiser and surer of myself. That makes my feelings for you wiser and surer by the same amount. It is a different emotion, as true champagne is different from the ersatz kind.'

She could only stare at him, hypnotised. 'Can I believe you?' she whispered.

'If you want to.' He smiled. 'As for your suspicions that Eva still hankers after me, you could not be further from the truth. Eva is fond of me, in her shallow way, but she has no romantic feelings left, I assure you. Besides which, she has a coterie of very devoted suitors at Lipari, including an American movie producer who makes me look like a pauper. She will enjoy herself for the next year or two, picking her next husband, and will then settle down to a life of unrestrained hedonism.'

'Oh, Xavier, I'm so sorry. I'm so sorry about the car, about everything——'

The entrance of the nurse with two doctors interrupted her words. Xavier rose, touching her cheek. 'This is where I have to leave,' he said.

'Please,' she begged him frantically, her fingers twining around his, 'don't go far! When will I see you?'

'As soon as they'll let me.' He rubbed his jaw wearily. 'I need a shave, a bath and a hot meal. They tell me I can get all that downstairs. I won't be far, I promise.'

What they had to do to her broken arm was agonisingly painful, yet she didn't care how much they hurt her.

The sense of relief and happiness inside her was overwhelming—an utterly selfish joy in knowing that her husband cared about her. Out of the nightmare of loneliness and self-deception a jewel had been born, and she wore that jewel deep in her heart.

Its radiance was starting to flood her being, making her, as one doctor had remarked with amusement, 'the happiest multiple fracture case on Ward Twelve.'

Within two days they let her get out of bed, and move around with the aid of a crutch on one side, and Xavier on the other. He took her down the spotlessly clean corridor to the little balcony at the end that looked out over a courtyard. Below them, palms rustled in the sunshine, and a big medlar tree was already starting to make fruit.

'I've said things to you, awful things, that I've bitterly regretted ever since.' She looked up, and saw his handsome face intent on hers. 'I've treated you as though you were some kind of monster.' She winced at the memory of her own attitude to him. 'I've behaved unforgivably.'

'You only spoke as you believed,' Xavier said quietly, his eyes probing her own, as though seeking the truth there.

'No,' she said, shaking her head firmly. 'I've never believed half the things I've said to you. If you could just believe that I somehow wasn't in my right mind, you might find it easier to forgive me.'

'It's never difficult to forgive you,' he said with a shadowy smile. 'But I, too, have made unforgivable mistakes. Like being so harsh with you at first, letting my hurt and anger get the better of my compassion, just at the time when I should have been most understanding. I've been such a fool, Romy. And when I think how I nearly lost you . . .'

Romy felt her heart contract at his expression. 'You don't want to lose me any more, do you?' she asked gently.

He shook his head with a half-smile. 'No, Romy. I don't want to lose another second of your company ever again.

When you spoke of leaving me, of getting a divorce, I just couldn't stop myself from lashing out at you. I felt that if I had to lock you in the tower I would have done!'

'I'm very flattered.' She laughed unsteadily.

'I'm only a man, not a saint. And you never guessed how much I really cared for you.' His voice became rough. 'I was still not mature when Eva and I divorced. When things didn't work out with you, the hurt was far, far worse. Worse because my feelings were so much deeper, and my capacity for hurt so much greater. Worse because with you there was so much yet to discover and achieve together. I knew that my marriage with you would bring more joy and fulfilment than my marriage to Eva could ever have done. And then, all that hope seemed to be in danger of destruction.' His face tightened. 'I felt bitterness and anger fill me. I was obsessed with keeping you with me, even at the cost of making you my prisoner, and losing your love.'

'If I'd known all that . . .' Her voice tailed off hopelessly.

'How could you? I'd never told you. Maybe I was wrong to wait for so long. But my damned pride got in the way. I couldn't bear the thought of being rejected by you, of having you laugh in my face.' He met her eyes. 'It's taken us a long time to get these things said, hasn't it?'

'Yes,' she whispered. 'But I'm very glad we've done it. There's no way you can undo the past, Xavier. But the future is infinitely more important. Don't you think?'

'Yes,' he said, drawing her close. 'Our future is very important, Romy. There is nothing that has greater importance to me.'

Three days later, she and Xavier emerged under the colonnade of palm trees in the florid hospital gardens. She had been discharged with a caution not to put any strain on her broken arm for at least a month.

'Come on,' she urged, as he paused to look back over his

shoulder. 'I hate hospitals.'

'So do I. But I can't help feeling rather fond of this one.' He took her arm with a smile, and led her to the waiting Daimler. 'The sea is just a kilometre away,' he said. 'What about a walk on the beach, a *very* expensive lunch with champagne, and then a slow drive home?'

'That would be marvellous,' she consented eagerly.

'Hmm.' He was incredibly handsome today. The beautiful camel sweater set his dark looks off to perfection; like so many Italian men, Xavier had an instinctive dress sense that made him look effortlessly elegant, whether his clothes were casual or formal. He turned to give her a quick glance from under black eyebrows. 'You're not very talkative.'

'I'm just happy,' she said, reaching out to caress his shoulder. He didn't just look good. He felt good, smelt good; he filled her life with happiness and excitement.

They reached the beach. The sea was deep blue, the sky almost cloudless overhead. It was hard to believe this was the dead of winter over the rest of Europe.

They walked a short way on the clean and solitary sand, then went to the edge of the sea, where the blue waves lapped gently. Out on the calm water, several yachts were drifting, defying the cold air.

Xavier stopped her, and reached out to brush the blowing hair away from her cheeks, cupping her face. 'How's the arm?' he asked, his eyes searching hers.

'Good as new. But if I'm not wrong, you were about to kiss me?'

Xavier studied her face with bright grey eyes for a moment. His deeply carved mouth looked as though it was on the edge of breaking into a smile. 'Do you know how you make me feel?'

Romy reached up to put her good hand over his, her face flushed with happiness. 'I have some idea.'

'Some idea . . .' He kissed her with a passion that took her breath away, his mouth telling her in no uncertain terms what he wanted to do to her. 'You mean so much to me,' he said huskily.

They stood locked in a tight embrace for a long while, just drinking in the contact with each other's bodies.

When he released her, his expression was serious. 'While you've been in hospital, I've had time to think about many things,' he said quietly. 'Many things that I now regret very bitterly. Most of all, perhaps, I regret the way I lied to you. I was insane to try a trick like that. I should have told you that I loved you, and tried to convince you of the truth, instead of being put off by your hostility. You see, I felt that the rest would follow, once you were my wife. I thought I would be able to tell you the truth later on. I didn't imagine that you had the force of will to cling to your delusions so strongly, and for so long.'

She laid her head against his chest for support, feeling his arms slide round her, his hand stroking her hair. The feeling in her was an alloy of pain and pleasure, of desire and joy.

'I really thought I had lost you when you finally found out the truth. It took me a long time to forget that look in your eyes that morning.'

Romy shuddered. 'I was half crazy that morning.'

'I had no inkling of how you would react. I didn't anticipate that you'd want to go back to England. As usual, I had underestimated the force of your passions. I could not believe that I could feel so much for you, and you so little for me. Or so little that was good. It maddened me to see you expending so much energy in hate, when I felt that you had such a powerful capacity for love. I felt that if I didn't hold you to me with chains of steel, you would go, and I would lose you for ever. So again I had to lie. I had to become an iron man, even though my heart was bleeding for you. If I'd shown the slightest weakness, you'd have slipped through my fingers.' His eyes reflected some of the darkness he'd been through. 'At that time, all you respected was force, power. If I'd shown you compassion, you would have despised me.'

'I think I would,' she said, recognising his insight into her character. 'Oh, Xavier,' she mumbled, 'I'm so very sorry . . .'

Xavier laughed raggedly. 'There is nothing to be sorry about any more. Neither of us has been shining models of understanding. I should have given you so much more comfort than I did. I should have helped you, supported you——'

'You *tried*.' She couldn't bear to hear him blame himself. 'You tried again and again, but you couldn't get near me. I wouldn't let you.'

'We are both cursed with pride,' he said in a wry voice. 'Perhaps it's our Sicilian blood.'

'Can we ever cancel out the past?' she whispered, her head against his chest. 'I've been so wrong about you. Wrong about your character, and your reasons for marrying me. I had this unshakeable conviction that you simply wanted heirs for your title . . .'

'I want a family,' he said, giving the word a slight emphasis. 'I am past thirty, Romy. At my age, a man starts to think about such things. I don't want to be an old man by the time my sons and daughters grow up. Heirs? That's an old-fashioned word which doesn't hold much warmth. I want children, Romy. *Your* children.'

'And I,' she replied in a whisper, 'want *your* children. As soon as possible. I want to see you with our baby in your arms . . .'

He stared at her, as though seeing her for the first time. 'I never thought I'd hear you say that,' he declared.

'Xavier,' she said quietly. 'I've changed so much. I sometimes wonder if you know quite how much. You've had a horrible time with me. Why you just didn't drown me in the sea I'll never know. On the day you married me, I was a child. I was a blind, miserable, spoiled child, and I felt like an animal in a trap. I'm not a child any more. I'm a woman. And I'm your wife. And I want so much to do what's right . . .'

'What is this?' he smiled. 'A repentance?'

'No,' she said simply. 'I think it's more a declaration . . . of love . . .'

Xavier's reaction was unaffectedly joyous. Before she quite knew what was happening, he had swept her up in his arms and swung her in a dizzy circle, so that the sunlit beach and the glittering blue sea blurred into bright colours around her.

'I didn't think that word existed in your vocabulary,' he said, as he let her down to earth again.

'Love?' she said with a gasping laugh. 'Oh, it does, now. I just regret that it's taken me so long to learn the meaning of it.'

'You haven't even started learning,' he assured her, his eyes brilliant with happiness. 'You're going to spend the rest of your life filling in the details . . .'

He smiled and kissed her mouth, tall and handsome, easily the most wonderful-looking man she'd ever set eyes on. She looked into his eyes, eyes so deep and warm that they could flood her being, drowning her will in his spirit. 'Have I ever told you,' she asked breathlessly, 'how utterly, irrevocably gorgeous you are?'

'You've said something of the sort,' he reminded her with a grin. 'But you can tell me again, if you really insist. I'm very vain.'

'I'll save it until we get back,' she said with a husky laugh.

There were no more barriers between them now. Romy knew with utter certainty that she had found love, that in this potent, dark man who had chosen her as his wife she had met the destiny for which she had been born. Love, more love, and yet more love were the only prospects on her horizon; a life as rich and fulfilled as it had once promised to be desolate and bleak.

She had no more delusions about Xavier. She had come to understand him for what he was: the most perfect man she would ever know. And what she had been struggling and fighting and rebelling against for the past months had been not him, but herself. It had taken a leap within her own imagination, an understanding of her own inner self, to make the scales drop from her eyes. And the truth she had found was precious and beautiful . . .

They ate lunch in a restaurant overlooking the sea, and set off homeward. The suburbs of Catania sped by, and within half an hour, they were driving through the wild, rugged hills of the Sicilian heartland, heading towards Luca.

Curled up in the seat beside him, she could hardly take her eyes off him. How incredible to think that this man was her husband. This magnificent pagan, this superb mind, this overwhelming lover, was her own—and she was his. That he had chosen her, out of all the women in the world, was like a miracle to her sometimes.

'How long have you wanted to marry me?'

'A long time.' He smiled gently. 'Ever since I realised that the spoiled little beauty with the deep blue eyes was the only woman I would ever love.'

'I gave you a merry chase, didn't I?'

'But I knew you would be mine, one day. It was just a question of being patient. You made me wait a long time, though.'

'You'll never have to wait again! I was terrified of you, you know,' she informed him.

'No. You were in love. But you were too young to know it.'

'Too stupid, you mean. You're right, though. I've loved

you ever since I was a child. It was my own feelings that frightened me. Oh, Xavier, I regret Paul Mortimer so much . . .'

'Don't. I know you went through pain because of him. But pain is necessary in life, just as joy is. I believe that we are allotted a ration of both. It strikes me as wonderful that we have both passed through our period of pain, my love. I know that only joy awaits us from now on.'

'If it's in my power,' she vowed quietly, 'you'll never feel another pang as long as you live.'

'And I make the same promise to you,' he smiled. He braked unexpectedly, and pulled the car to a halt by the side of the road.

'No petrol?' she purred, reaching for him. 'How convenient.'

'Patience, you wanton.' He grinned. 'I want to show you something. Come on, get out.'

She followed him in perplexity. The road was deserted, running in a winding ribbon through farmland. She slid her arm round his waist, and followed his pointing finger.

Her eyes widened. At first she thought the tree in the field had been decked with white lace, as for a wedding.

Then she realised that its dark branches were covered with a delicate foam of snowy blossom.

'It's an almond,' she whispered. 'The almond blossom is out!'

'Yes.' He nodded. 'The spring is here.'

'I love you,' she said quietly. 'You're all the world to me.'

'And I love you.' He kissed her lips. 'I'll always love you, Romy. I always have.'

And beyond the little tree was another, also in bloom—and another, and another. And as her eyes travelled to the horizon, towards her home, the earth seemed to be covered in the fragrant white and pink flowers, an incontrovertible promise of the new hope and new life to come.

Have You Ever Wondered If You Could Write A Harlequin Novel?

Here's great news—Harlequin is offering a series of cassette tapes to help you do just that. Written by Harlequin editors, these tapes give practical advice on how to make your characters—and your story—come alive. There's a tape for each contemporary romance series Harlequin publishes.

Mail order only

All sales final

TO: **_Harlequin Reader Service_**
Audiocassette Tape Offer
P.O. Box 1396
Buffalo, NY   14269-1396

I enclose a check/money order payable to HARLEQUIN READER SERVICE® for $9.70 ($8.95 plus 75¢ postage and handling) for EACH tape ordered for the total sum of $_____*
Please send:

☐ Romance and Presents   ☐ Intrigue
☐ American Romance   ☐ Temptation
☐ Superromance   ☐ All five tapes ($38.80 total)

Signature_____
                                                        (please print clearly)
Name:_____

Address:_____

State:_____ Zip:_____

*Iowa and New York residents add appropriate sales tax.

AUDIO-H